R. J. Antanaitis

ALL SAINTS PLAY

iUniverse, Inc.
Bloomington

All Saints Play

This is a work of fiction. All of the characters, names, incidents, organizations, and dialogue in this novel are either the products of the author's imagination or are used fictitiously.

iUniverse books may be ordered through booksellers or by contacting:

iUniverse
1663 Liberty Drive
Bloomington, IN 47403
www.iuniverse.com
1-800-Authors (1-800-288-4677)

ISBN: 978-1-4620-3161-0 (sc)
ISBN: 978-1-4620-3162-7 (e)
ISBN: 978-1-4620-3163-4 (dj)

Library of Congress Control Number: 2011910884

Printed in the United States of America

iUniverse rev. date: 8/25/2011

Note/Disclaimer: There are numerous paraphrased references to the Bible.

To Elizabeth

Contents

Author's Note

NEW ORLEANS HAS BEEN the home of the New Orleans Saints football team since 1967. During the first year of their existence, the Saints won three games and lost eleven, matching the best win-loss record of any expansion team during its first year. Prior to the 2009–10 football season, the best year the Saints ever had was during the 1987–88 season, when they finished the regular season with twelve wins and three losses. That season they lost the wild-card game to the Minnesota Vikings by a score of forty-four to ten. The Saints were crushed, physically and spiritually. The football team had existed for over forty years, but they had never been to the Super Bowl.

Then came 2010. Perhaps the year had finally arrived for some famous down-home "Cajun cooking" way down south in N'awlins. During the War of 1812, the American troops were led by Major General Andrew Jackson, and they defeated the British army in the final major battle of the war. I wondered what would happen if only Andrew Jackson could somehow step through a time warp from 1812 or if Jesus Christ could return to earth and lead the way to victory in one of the most significant battles in which the city of New Orleans had ever participated. If Jackson were alive in 2010, he might be the very first person to truly believe the Saints could actually win the Super Bowl.

(NOTE: After this book was written, the New Orleans Saints won their first Super Bowl in February 2010. Congratulations to the Saints for this phenomenal accomplishment!)

Prologue

TEARS ARE LIQUID DROPLETS cascading from the soul. In early January of the year AD 2010, J. C. De Lord was saddened by the thought that his disciples had forgotten him. About two thousand years ago, J. C. came to Earth to perform something miraculous so that the "saints" would continue to believe in him.

Toward the end of his first visit here, J. C. had supper with friends near the Garden of Gethsemane and then went into the garden by himself to pray. J. C. was well aware that that night might very well be his last on Earth and that he was soon destined to meet his fate. "His sweat was as if it were great drops of blood falling down upon the ground" (Luke 22:44). An angel came from heaven and sat nearby to provide him with strength. J. C. thought, *Before long, this garden will be a garden of tears, and I shall receive the kiss of death from a friend.* A lonely tear began its fateful journey as it rolled down his cheek. He also realized the possibility existed for him to return to Earth in the distant future. J. C. walked to a corner of the garden and stood near an olive tree. He was burdened with extreme sadness but he suddenly had a random thought. He had a strange vision of playing in a new game, one called football, but he somehow understood that such a game wouldn't exist for another twenty centuries. He asked himself, *Are you ready for some football?* With just a trace of a smile, he then cleverly admonished himself, *You can't possibly play in a football game until there is a football!* He admired the beautiful flowers and was inspired by the sweet-smelling nectar. He inhaled and exhaled deeply several times, as if he were trying to capture the fragrant aroma forever. He was well aware that a tear had just trickled down his cheek, and it was followed by a sardonic smile. That morning he had awakened relatively early, as he was accustomed to, and he had walked to the marketplace just to "hang out" with some of his friends.

After J. C. arrived at the marketplace, his good friend Thomas showed up. It should be noted that Thomas's nickname was Didymus, or Diddio, which was conceivably a precursor to the word "Daddio," a term of endearment during the beatnik or hippie era of the 1960s. J. C. acknowledged Thomas's presence and asked, "What's new, Brother Diddio?" J. C. and Diddio began to speak with some of the other merchants and tax collectors.

In our modern-day society, no one goes to see a tax collector voluntarily. Tax collectors send you bills in the mail and we all know it would be for the best if bills are paid in full in a timely manner. Tax collectors don't necessarily beat you like they did centuries ago, but they are still quite capable of making your life miserable.

J. C. decided he would take advantage of his inalienable rights, which included his right to free speech. There were a number of people in the crowd who didn't necessarily agree that he had the right to exercise free speech. Nonetheless, he decided to preach his thoughts and recommendations. When he spoke his mind, a lot of people didn't agree with him, and they became quite agitated. During J. C.'s lengthy harangue, Diddio made it explicitly clear that he doubted or didn't necessarily concur with some of J. C.'s thoughts and expostulations. J. C. remained adamant and advocated that his rationale could change the world. Like a lot of politicians and orators, he proposed that "change" would be a good thing. Several times, J. C. proffered a concept, and Peter, another friend who had shown up, told him right to his face, "Are you kidding, man? I don't know you. I don't know you. I just don't know you!" Another more distant associate named Judast had consorted with some people who clearly did not embrace J. C.'s way of thinking. Judast had decided he could even make a few bucks if he helped his business associates take J. C. under their jurisdiction. Several hours later, after dinner, the local police force arrived and attempted to place J. C. under arrest for no apparent reason. Peter continued to make it quite clear that he had nothing to do with J. C. and didn't know him. Diddio had already faded away into the crowd.

In a New York minute, J. C. found himself in front of a judge and executioner, a man quick to make important decisions. J. C. was not provided with legal counsel, and he did not have a jury of his peers. The judge asked a vast crowd of people if they wanted J. C. released back into society (where he would probably continue to speak his mind) or if they wanted some local thug named Big Abbas to be granted a pardon, perhaps as a reward for recently demonstrating some good behavior. No one was there to count the votes. There were no malfunctioning machines with "chads." As the people in the crowd cheered and clapped, no one had any special electronic equipment to determine the highest decibel level to help decide whether J. C. or Big Abbas should be exonerated and set free. Anyway, the judge was influenced by the crowd, and he made a decision that altered the course of mankind. The judge decided that J. C would be removed permanently from the marketplace, after which he would be forced to carry a large wooden beam through the streets.

J. C. commented, "I have preached to others. Help us all, that we do not run like a man running aimlessly" (Corinthians 9:26) Suddenly, J. C. looked around and realized all of his good buddies were essentially nowhere to be seen. J. C. accepted his fate and asked, "Where did they go?" Throughout the years that followed, he would ask that same question many times.

Please let me introduce myself before I go on. I am a spiritual being. My name is Bubba, and I am proud to be an angel. I have never met another angel named Bubba. I am the narrator and guide for this story. I have been an angel for about ten years. When I was an earthly being, I was raised right smack in the middle of Louisiana, where I played football and explored the bayous. During that life, I managed to get into my fair share of trouble, and I never acted like an angel. I played offensive tackle in high school and college, and one of my primary responsibilities was to protect the quarterback at all times, both on and off the field. Not long ago, God called me over to AHQ (Angel Headquarters) and told me that J. C. was going to do something special on Super Bowl Sunday and that he, God, needed me to stay in the background and watch over J. C.

I can't be seen but I can be heard. I can communicate with J. C., and he can communicate with me.

I am going to tell you about a miraculous football game and other events surrounding it, with some of my personal opinions sprinkled in along the way. It seems like every angel has his or her personal opinions. So, let the story begin.

Recently

J. C. SAT DOWN by himself, and his gaze immediately affixed upon a nearby cloud that seemed incredibly close. The cloud swirled lazily and aimlessly. J. C. thought, *What a heavenly view this is.*

J. C. and his father had decided that a very long time had elapsed since his last visit. It seemed like eons. There were many reasons to visit and many reasons not to visit. They debated whether J. C. should visit a couple of sheepherders in a remote village in Tibet or someone named Bruno in the Bronx. Maybe he should attend a significant event like the final baseball game in the World Series in late October. J. C.'s father finally concluded that J. C. should make a guest appearance as a player at the next Super Bowl, which had already been scheduled for early February in Miami, Florida. It would be Super Bowl XLIV. J. C. shrugged his shoulders and agreed that Super Bowl Sunday would be acceptable to him.

One day, during another lengthy conversation with his father, J. C. offered, "Some people will probably question why I would appear at a football game instead of being there for an earthquake, tornado, or hurricane. It's too bad that people don't understand that the almighty powers do not sit around and concoct natural disasters or bus, train, or aircraft accidents. There will be occasions when a cat falls out of a tree and does not land on its feet, and there will be times when a polar bear will fall through a chunk of ice and drown. Throughout the universe, the weather and atmospheric conditions change periodically. As a result, Mother Nature decides whether people are going to have a sunny day, a cloudy day, or another type of day altogether." J. C. focused on his two scarred palms and added, "Things happen in life, and I am well aware of this fact, as I experienced it during my human existence." J. C.'s father reminded him that if he returned to Earth, anything could happen.

J. C. walked away from his father and sat by himself. As far as he could remember, he had always been able to make quick and incisive decisions. J. C. occasionally spoke out loud when there was no one else around who could hear him. He exclaimed, "I'm going to the Super Bowl! There will be thousands of people there, and the game will be watched by millions of people all over the world." Then he suddenly shouted, "Are you ready for some football?" He responded calmly, "Yes, I am." He consistently kept himself in good shape, so there would be no need to work out or lift weights or run long distances. He was ready to go. He was ready to play. He thought about how football teams work extremely hard for many months to earn a victory. He also thought there would be no need for any pomp or circumstance when he showed up for the game. The only thing his team would have to do would be to score one more point than the other team.

Without much further thought, he determined the game should be an exciting one. It would not be a game which had a final score of ninety to zero. J. C. stood up abruptly and declared, "I have to go make plans for Miami! I'm going to the Super Bowl!" He tugged slightly on his right earlobe with his thumb and index finger. The nearby clouds became agitated, almost as if they were initiating plans of their own as they whirled off in a purposeful direction.

J.C. Arrives at
Sun Life Stadium

J. C. DE LORD, dressed in a plain T-shirt and faded blue jeans, stood with his arms folded on the sidewalk near an intersection just a few hundred yards from Sun Life Stadium (the home of the Miami Dolphins football team). J. C. said he only had three words for me, "Bubba, we're here." He had never played football before, but he was focused on his imminent transformation into a professional football player. J. C. had to make his way into the locker room to suit up for the game. At first glance, it appeared that J.C De Lord was nondescript. Closer scrutiny revealed he was about six feet one, weighed approximately 190 pounds, and possessed an athletic physique. He had piercing light-blue eyes, dark-brown hair, and a short, well-kempt beard that was about half a shade lighter than the hair on top of his head. If you looked closely, there were long-healed scars on the palms of his hands, the tops of his feet, and the upper part of his forehead. Most women would consider him fairly attractive.

The kickoff for Super Bowl XLIV was about an hour away. It had been a dark and stormy afternoon, but this was not unusual weather for Miami, Florida, in early February.

There were thousands of people milling about. It was as if Sun Life Stadium was the beehive and all the people were the bees. There was incessant buzzing coupled with perpetual motion both in and around the "hive." Ticket scalpers were trying to sell tickets at prices so high that most people would have to take out a second mortgage to be able to buy them. It was late afternoon, and J. C. gazed up toward the heavens and spoke softly to himself, "The weather should really be better than this. Mother always said if you don't like the way something is, then fix it." He looked up, and the clouds twirled and shifted and began to drift off into the distance. Only a few minutes elapsed before bursting rays of sunshine brightened the sky and a full, resplendent rainbow appeared. From where J. C. stood, the stadium was perfectly centered at the bottom of the rainbow, and the structure gleamed and sparkled like a colorful kaleidoscope.

To be more specific, it was about five o'clock on a Sunday afternoon in early February. As the storm front dissipated, the air was filled with eager anticipation that it would, in fact, turn out to be a picture-perfect evening for Super Bowl XLIV. The football field remained wet and slippery from the earlier rainfall, and it was still windy enough to be slightly bothersome. It was still beautiful. As some people put it, Miami in February is "God's country," and the way the afternoon was turning out was proving them right.

During the past several weeks, it seemed that every newspaper and sporting magazine in the world had been saturated with articles and stories explaining how the football season, which began in September 2009, had already turned into a miraculous one for the New Orleans Saints football team. After the city of New Orleans battled courageously with Hurricane Katrina during the fall of 2005, the Saints' recent performance was embraced by old and new fans alike. After losing their first two games of the season, they marched on audaciously to win twelve consecutive games. Then they suddenly managed to lose their last two regular season games, proving that they were mere mortals after all. The Saints' overall record of twelve wins and four losses was the best in the NFC, and it earned them a bye—essentially a week off—in the first round of the playoffs.

During the second week of playoff games, the Saints surged to a 14–0 halftime lead over the Dallas Cowboys and then managed to hold on for a hard-fought 17–13 victory. In their next game, the Saints found themselves trailing the Chicago Bears by a score of 27–14 at the end of the third quarter. To make a long story short, a seventy-three-yard return of a blocked punt and a forty-seven-yard touchdown pass with only twenty-four seconds left on the game clock enabled the Saints to overcome the thirteen point deficit and win the game with a score of 28–27.

This took the Saints to exactly where they wanted to be. They found themselves on their way to the Super Bowl for the very first time in the franchise's history. Was it remotely possible that the Saints could win this game of all games for themselves, for the National Football League, for the city of New Orleans, and for all of their faithful and faithless fans? In a way, the Saints had won the holy wars by being victorious in their first two playoff games. Now it was time for their greatest battle ever!

Some of the Saints: Peter, Thomas, and Jude

THREE OF THE SAINTS' most important players were Peter Rockport, the fullback, Thomas Allmen, a wide receiver, and Jude Thadley, a halfback. Jude was a friendly guy, and he was always in good spirits. He grew up on a cattle farm in Iowa with so many brothers and sisters that it was almost impossible to account for them all. For some reason, his mother seemed to have difficulty remembering all of their names. She would call out for Billy when she really wanted Bobby. Jude's specialty on the farm was baling hay. As a young teenager, he acquired the nickname "Hay Jude," and it stuck with him for the rest of his life. If he was given the football and had just a little bit of room, he would make the best of it and gain some yardage. Every single time he ran with the ball, the crowd would chant "Hay Jude," and it always sounded as if the crowd were singing. Over time, Jude gained a reputation for making impossible catches and for gaining positive yardage, especially in desperate situations. He had one of the best pickup lines ever, and only he could use it. He would approach a pretty girl and say, "Hay, I'm your man."

The unquestionable foundation of the team was Peter "Rocky" Rockport. Rocky was a stalwart. You could always hear Rocky saying, "You can count on me, count on it, and count me in." Rocky grew up in a small Texas town with two younger siblings, a brother and a sister. He lived in a nice house and had a perfect family. When he was fourteen years old, his father died unexpectedly. Even though there was a sizeable life insurance policy, Rocky immediately assumed the role of "man of the house." He possessed an innate mechanical ability. He was born to nurture and take care of others. He assumed total responsibility for mowing the lawn and all other household chores, both inside and out. He took good care of his mother, brother, and sister. The day he turned sixteen, he sought and found employment at both the local hardware store and the supermarket. He immediately began to work forty to fifty hours per week, but he still attained excellent grades and was on the high school wrestling team and the football team, where he played fullback. If there was a critical play and the team needed a yard, they could count on Rocky to gain two yards or more. He was reliable, dependable, conscientious, and he was an Eagle Scout. Rocky eventually went to an Ivy League university with both academic and athletic scholarships, and he graduated magna cum laude. It seemed like a relatively high percentage of Rocky's classmates had relatives who had previously attended Ivy League schools. Rocky didn't, and his graduation day brought great joy to his mother.

Rocky was the Saints' fullback, and he wore the number twenty-nine on his jersey. The summer before the 2009–10 season, he was signed by the Saints after playing in the Canadian Football League. Rocky was a brute, at six feet four and 240 pounds. He was a difficult runner to tackle despite the fact that he was bowlegged. He always joked that God had bent his legs "just right," and this allowed him to maintain extremely good balance. Whenever Rocky ran with the football, he ran just one way, directly downfield toward the goal line. Shortly after being signed by the Saints, he met several of the other players, including Thomas Allmen.

Thomas Allmen was raised in Indiana by a stay-at-home mom and a father who worked as a laborer in a nearby factory. Thomas always had a special relationship with his sister, Faith. He teased her all the time, but he loved her. His parents loved them both but were not demonstrative with their love. There always seemed to be enough food on the table, but there was never much money left for nonnecessities. He worked hard in school. Sometimes he achieved very good grades, As and Bs, and sometimes he ended up with Cs and Ds. The grade he got usually depended upon how much he liked the subject matter or the teacher. And even though he worked hard, he was always doubtful that he could write a paper or do well on a test. He was also doubtful about relationships with other people and about his athletic capabilities. He was always a pessimistic guy. This characteristic was embedded into his personality, despite the fact that he had so many things going for him. He doubted that anything would ever work or come out well in the end. Thomas earned a football scholarship to a prominent college, where he was a starter for all four years, and he matriculated with a degree in business administration.

Thomas was a man who had very little faith in almost anything he did or thought about. Every day of the year, he woke up and said, "I doubt that today will be a good one." He played the position of wide receiver for the Saints, and he was absolutely convinced that his team could never win the Super Bowl. Although he was a person of "little faith," he was the Saint who was most obsessed with turning the fortunes of the team around. Every single day he fantasized about the New Orleans Saints winning the Super Bowl. He also dedicated time every day to deep meditation and prayers for the Saints to be successful. He couldn't really explain why he did this. He finally concluded that he must be possessed by either a good spirit or an evil spirit. Thomas had been a Saint for several years, and he thought constantly about what he or his teammates could do to make the Saints a better team. He thought of new and innovative offensive plays and shared them with the team's offensive coordinator, who was actually receptive to some of his suggestions.

Thomas was well aware that his team was one of only a few that had never yet been to a Super Bowl. During the past three seasons, it had become painfully obvious to Thomas that the Saints would not get to the Super Bowl and that the only way he would see the game would be to watch it on television. This year finally provided a glimmer of hope to his dreams and aspirations. After the team reeled off several consecutive victories, Thomas began to believe the Saints could win it all this season. To Thomas, this would be a feat bordering on the miraculous, as he routinely thought that nothing good could ever happen in his life.

Thomas was blondish with a light complexion. He was six feet one and 210 pounds. He was a wide receiver and wore a jersey with the number three on it. He was a veteran; this was his third year with the Saints. Although he could be social in a crowd, he was generally a loner. He was a thinker. He loved to read books and do crossword puzzles. Whenever he ran with a football, he ran with a darting motion, here and there and everywhere. He went to the left, he went to the right, and then he went back to the left. He was fast, tricky, and elusive. He knew what he wanted to do, but at the same time, he often didn't know how he wanted to do it. He constantly changed his mind. He couldn't decide what he wanted for lunch. Thank God he had his Faith, his sister, to help him buy clothes, furniture, and accessories for his apartment. In fact, she often helped Thomas make final decisions, which on some days even included the selection of a sandwich.

Faith was one of life's faithful fans. She was an avid fan of the New Orleans Saints. One reason for this was that her twin brother, Thomas, played on the team. Another reason was that she worked at a casino in Biloxi, Mississippi, for a couple of years following her graduation from college. It was Faith's perception that a large percentage of the people who lived in Mississippi rooted for the Saints. She understood that you actually had to live there for at least a year before you could even come close to being able to pronounce the word Biloxi correctly. Faith always acknowledged that it was difficult to do, but she believed it should sound something like "Baluxxi" or "Bluxxi." As soon as she came closer to the proper pronunciation, the locals began to embrace and befriend her. During her time in Mississippi, she had developed a deep love for the Saints. She came to understand that it is challenging for a person to faithfully follow a sports team that has not played well historically and does not have a respectable win-loss record. She understood that you somehow have to dig down deep into your heart and soul to continue to follow and support a team like the Saints. Despite the fact that she had witnessed many agonizing defeats, she continued to believe that things could only get better. She was always convinced that the team would win its next game. Even though she didn't see positive results, she continued to believe. There are so many fans throughout the world that faithfully

9

support losing teams for decades. If asked, a lot of these fans would say their team will probably lose the next game, but they somehow concurrently believe in the deepest recesses of their souls that their team will definitely win the next game. All sports fans are well aware that there is always next year.

Faith had always been there for Thomas. She was a sister and a friend. She and her mother were the only ones that called him "Tommie." Although Faith and Thomas were twins, they had different birthdays. Thomas was born at 11:16 p.m. on July 3 and Faith became an Independence Day baby when she was born forty-six minutes later at 12:02 a.m. on July 4. Their parents always recalled Faith's fifth birthday vividly. The cake was on the table, the candles were lit, and it was time for Faith to blow them out. She realized it would be challenging for her and remembered how easily Tommie had extinguished his candles the day before. She walked directly to Tommie, grabbed him by the hand, and escorted him closer to the cake, where she directed him, "Tommie, help me blow out the candles!" She reminded him that he had had his feast the day before and now it was time for her to blow out her candles. And blow out the candles they did. From that moment, both she and Thomas realized that one of the reasons Faith had been born was to help Thomas make appropriate decisions in life, because he sometimes had difficulty doing so all by himself. Faith was always optimistic about everything. She always believed that every single day would be perfect and wonderful.

Thomas was faithless and Faith was faithful, and they melded together to form a most harmonious, loving, and supportive relationship.

Thomas didn't plan on introducing Rocky to Faith. It just happened. On an off-day in August, Thomas was eating lunch with Faith in a sub shop, and Rocky, one of his new teammates, walked in. Thomas invited Rocky to join them. Rocky saw Faith and quickly concluded that he should try his best to be a gentleman and not talk with his mouth full and not spill any special sauce on the front of his shirt. The next day, Rocky had lunch with Faith again and realized subconsciously that he would always have Faith in his life.

At first, Thomas didn't know what he thought about the budding relationship between Rocky and his sister. He only wanted whatever was best for Faith. He began to bond with Rocky, both on the field and off. In the back of his mind, he knew that Rocky was a great guy and his evolving relationship with Faith was a match made in heaven. Rocky and Thomas became lifelong friends; they both knew they could always count on one another.

Rocky was no saint, and he had dated several attractive girls. He once picked up a girl for a first date, and about ten minutes later he told her that he had a bad headache and took her home. She was attractive but had a voice that sounded like chalk screeching across a blackboard. There were a couple of girls he thought he really liked, and he dated them for several weeks. For reasons he couldn't verbalize, the relationships didn't last. Then Rocky met Faith, and it changed his life forever. He knew he liked her from the start. Within just a couple of days, he found himself thinking about her as he was trying to go to sleep at night. He thought about her as he was waking up. He thought about her all day long. His thoughts and emotions emanated from his inner being. In a sense, they weren't logical thoughts. It was hard to explain, but his thoughts, feelings, and emotions somehow blended together into a romantic quandary. He just wanted to see Faith, to be with her, to hold her hand, to gaze into her enrapturing eyes. He thought of her and felt elated and queasy at the same time. Thoughts of her brightened his days and his nights.

It wasn't long before he realized that he was falling in love with her. This had never happened to him before.

He constantly thought about calling her and then made up stupid reasons to do so. He determined that he should act like a mature adult, but he consistently acted more childish. He thought he shouldn't be too forward. He tried to retain his overall composure but failed miserably. He couldn't concentrate when he tried to memorize football plays or watch game tapes. He couldn't focus when he tried to watch television or read a newspaper. He concluded that although love might be a many-splendored thing, it was also annoying. He wasn't himself. Sometimes hours would pass and he would accomplish virtually nothing at all. This wasn't like him. Other times, several hours would go by before he realized that he was hungry or thirsty. It occurred to him that he might starve to death if he wasn't careful.

Rocky was in love. It felt like a very active butterfly had snuck into his abdominal cavity and was flitting around with no specific destination in mind. For no apparent reason, he would feel his pulse racing and his heart throbbing in his chest. He felt there was joy and happiness in just about everything he did. There was a bounce in his step and a song in his heart. He seemed to have more energy and vitality than ever before. When he entered a room and saw Faith, he hardly noticed anything else in the room. During football practices, he would be tackled and immediately jump up off the ground with a big smile on his face. It really isn't normal for a person to get up from the ground with a grin after his body has just been driven to the ground by a jarring tackle. His teammates began to think that he was somewhat psychotic.

Rocky was in love. More than ever before, Rocky was aware of the birds, flowers, stars, sunshine, lollipops, and rainbows. Faith's presence awakened his inner soul. When he called her on the phone, she would ask why he called, and sometimes he had no good reason. The act of falling in love is a magical mystery. Falling in love is like smelling cinnamon for the very first time. It's like taking your very first bite of chocolate or your very first taste of ice cream. Within just a few days, Rocky was thinking, *How or why do I love her? Let me count the ways.* But there were so many ways that he had great difficulty trying to count them. He also realized there was nothing he could do to stop the momentum of his love.

Faith was about a year younger than Rocky. Although it is said that beauty is in the eye of the beholder, there was no doubt that Faith was a beautiful young woman. She had long, corn-silky blonde hair, sparkling blue eyes, an angelic face that was always filled with joy and zest for life, and a trim, athletic figure. She was not only pretty, she was also smart. She was a prelaw student on her way to a promising future. After she first met Rocky, she adjusted her busy schedule so she could see him more often. They spent an enormous amount of time together, and their relationship blossomed.

About three weeks after they first met, in the middle of September, Faith threw reason out the door and became obsessed with the thought of asking Rocky to marry her. Deep in her soul, she knew she was a traditional girl and would never do such a thing. But she was in love and didn't know what to do. Fortunately, Faith didn't have to wait long. The day after the thought entered her head, Rocky proposed to her. His proposal was a clever one. After dinner at his apartment, he asked Faith to stand about ten feet away from him. Rocky picked up a football and held it with his right hand and then placed the football on his chest near his heart. He then passed the football gently to Faith and said, "My dearest beloved, I pass you my heart. You are the girl for me for all eternity. Please marry me."

The tears welled in Faith's eyes and she exclaimed, "Touchdown! Yes, of course, my dearest love. I will marry you."

Rocky replied, "What are you doing? There is no crying in football!"

Three weeks into the relationship and there was already a marriage proposal. The sun was shining brightly every day and the birds were singing incessantly.

Early January: Way Down South in New Orleans

NEW ORLEANS IS A magical and exotic city. It's a city of the past, replete with history, but it also a city where people have dreams of a glorious future. It's the place where you'll find the infamous Bourbon Street. The city has tremendous jazz, pralines, steamboats on the Mississippi River, and the annual jazzed-up party that has no equal, Mardi Gras. Thomas Allmen and Rocky Rockport were out together on a Friday night in early January in New Orleans. They were accompanied by Faith, who had been Rocky's fiancé since the previous September. They were enjoying an early dinner, and they were seated next to a boisterous group of people. The three of them shared servings of dirty rice, gumbo, and jambalaya. They each had a Hurricane cocktail, and much to Faith's dismay, Rocky and Thomas had initiated a duel with the little umbrellas from their drinks. Just ten minutes earlier, Rocky had bought a bag of pralines for Faith. Initially, she had taken the position that she really didn't want them because they had too many calories. Ten minutes later, her staunch position regarding the pralines changed completely. Despite the fact that none of them had finished their meals, Faith grabbed the bag, opened it, and inhaled deeply. She exploded with laughter, "I thought we might have some King Cake for dessert, but I decided I'm going after some of these praline candies instead." She explained to Rocky how the candy was made with butter, sugar, cream, and pecans, all gloriously mixed together to form a gooey mess. After the candy hardened, the aroma was dangerously inviting.

Rocky teased her, "*Mon chéri*, you know you can't eat just one of those candies," and he playfully snatched the bag out of her hands. "I'm going to do you a favor and just eat the whole bag of candy by myself!"

Faith shouted, "Don't even go there. If you eat more than one of those pralines you're going to end up on Tchoupitoulas Street all by yourself." She attempted to pronounce it correctly, something almost no one was capable of doing. For some reason, she had a thing about pronouncing words correctly. She began to wrestle the bag out of Rocky's hands. He immediately gave up, smiled, and returned the entire bag of pralines to Faith. She took the bag and placed it down by her side so she could watch over it.

There was a whole lot of *gumbo ya-ya*—everybody talking all at once—going on. Faith listened and laughed out loud. She said, "I was just listening to the people at the next table." She did her best to use a proper Creole accent to explain. "They woke up this mornin' and found themselves sittin' in the bayou thinkin' about takin' the pirogue into the Big Easy to see the Ball. So they came to the City That Care Forgot and started walkin' down the banquette on Calliope Street because they were fixin' to head over to Fat City just to pass a good time and *laissez les bon temps rouler*." She added, "That's enough of that. I can't talk like that anymore; it's too much of an effort."

Thomas said, "There is no doubt about it. You got that right," while Rocky just shook his head back and forth and grinned.

Out of nowhere, Rudy Ruddast appeared at their table. He was another member of the Saints, and he played the position of offensive tackle. Rudy attempted to smile and placed his hands on the edge of the table and gave the standard New Orleans greeting, "Yat!" During the past few weeks, Rudy had attempted to flirt with Faith on several occasions, and she had not been receptive to his advances. Rudy was tall and was considered "devilishly handsome" in a sinister kind of way. He was one of the bad boys that some women are attracted to. Rudy didn't seem to have any close friends on the team, and he often ate meals by himself. He spent a lot of time on his cell phone. He made and received numerous telephone calls. The conversations were always brief, and no one ever knew who he was talking to. People occasionally saw him with a date, but no one ever saw him with the same girl twice.

Normally, there are approximately forty-five players on a professional football team. Rocky and Thomas did their best to get along with every teammate. Rocky really didn't have any strong feelings about Rudy, but Thomas had determined long ago that he just didn't like Rudy, though he couldn't explain why.

Faith seemed startled by Rudy's appearance. She replied, "Yat. The three of us are here having an early dinner. We're just about done, and we're ready to start diggin' into a bag of pralines. We sat down about an hour ago. It took some time, but I helped Rocky and Thomas order some unbelievable muffuletta sandwiches. Then they both changed their minds, and we decided to order some of this real Southern food instead." She was courteous, but her facial expression did not manifest any signs of warmth.

Thomas uttered something indistinguishable while Rocky greeted Rudy with an innocuous, "What's up, Bro?" as he continued to slurp his gumbo.

There were a few seconds of awkward silence after which Rudy said, "Well, I just saw you guys sittin' here, so I thought I would come over and say hello to a couple of my teammates and also offer a special hello to Faith." He continued, "Faith, it's very nice to see you today." Rudy didn't know that Rocky and Faith were a couple.

Faith stood up and responded curtly, "Thank you." Then she added, "Rudy, you arrived just as we were getting ready to leave. We have to run some errands. Bye. Maybe we'll see you later." Faith realized a few weeks earlier that Rudy was trying to hit on her, and it hadn't taken her long at all to determine that she just wasn't interested in him. In fact, whenever he was present she felt uncomfortable and did her best to avoid him.

Rudy didn't look at Rocky or Thomas. He looked directly at Faith and said, "I hope the three of you have a very nice day." He looked down at the table as his lips twisted into a wry smile, then he walked away.

Thomas said, "I have no comment!" Faith added that neither did she.

After leaving the restaurant, Rocky, Thomas, and Faith strolled down Bourbon Street, where they had a brief encounter with Hope Evig. Faith and Hope were good friends. Hope was with two other girls, and she saw Faith and the two men first. Hope approached them and exclaimed, "Yat! What brings you down to Bourbon Street this evening?" Faith and Hope embraced and pecked each other's cheek. They immediately began to exchange comments about each other's hair, fingernail polish, and shoes. Rocky and Thomas also exchanged pleasantries with Hope and then excused themselves to let the girls talk. They meandered about fifty feet away to watch a street performer.

Faith explained gleefully, "We had an early dinner. Now we're just munching on some pralines and walking around and watching all of the crazy stuff that happens around here. We're not staying out much longer. The guys have an early practice tomorrow morning."

Hope replied, "It sounds like you're having a good time. And that's good. Honey, I know you didn't forget that you and I have a super shopping spree scheduled for tomorrow morning and I will be over at your place at precisely 9:00 a.m. Don't forget to wear some really comfortable walking shoes!"

Faith laughed and said, "Sweetie Pie, just don't you worry none about me. When it comes to shopping, I can almost keep up with you!" Then they gave departing hugs and kisses on the cheeks, and Faith wandered over to stand next to the guys.

Faith Allmen and Hope Evig had been good friends for several years. They met at a team luncheon. Hope was the daughter of Mr. Charles Evig, one of the prestigious and wealthy owners of the New Orleans Saints. Hope was raised in New Orleans in a remodeled plantation home. Like most women, Hope loved to shop despite the fact that she had just about everything and anything that she ever needed or didn't need.

Hope was just a few months younger than Faith. When people looked at her they saw a tall, stunning blonde. In fact, some guys almost hurt their necks permanently turning to look at her as she passed them on a sidewalk or in a mall. She was a graduate of LSU but was not yet seriously interested in any kind of employment since her loving father was more than capable of keeping her collection of several dozen pocketbooks filled with spending money. She always dressed impeccably and looked like she could be on the cover of almost any magazine. Hope was a proper Southern belle and seemed to have the remarkable ability to turn the Southern accent and charm on and off like a light switch. She always seemed to be in a hurry to get somewhere even though she really didn't have any significant plans. When she went into a bank to get some spending money, she would address the men standing in line in front of her with the most charming Southern drawl that she could muster, saying something like, "Gentlemen, would y'all mind very much if I just scooted myself in front of you, because I am suddenly realizin' that I might be just a tad late for my hair appointment." It worked every time. Several men would jostle and bump into each other and do the best they could to get out of her way and let her go to the front of the line.

Approximately a year earlier, Hope had gone on a date with Rudy Ruddast one evening. Their date only lasted a few hours. It was a dinner date in an upscale restaurant, where they listened to some lively jazz. The following morning, Hope called Faith and told her everything. "Faith, last night I went out with Rudy Ruddast on a date. Only heaven knows why I agreed to go out with him in the first place. I just felt so uncomfortable with him. I just have to tell you, the dinner was a culinary delight. As soon as I finished my last mouthful of food, I excused myself and went to the ladies' room. Then I returned to the table and informed Rudy that my dinner apparently did not agree with me, and I asked to be taken home. I don't know why I did it, but I gave Rudy my cell phone number. But that's all he will ever get from me, and I assure you that I will never go on another date with that man. I don't know why, but he gives me the heebie-jeebies."

Faith and Hope always joked with each other. Faith said, "I have Hope."

Hope said, "I have Faith." They both said they didn't need anything else.

About a week elapsed, and it was mid-January. One night it just happened. Faith caught some strain of a European flu bug. She battled it overnight, at home, by herself. The next morning she lay in her bed, motionless. When she failed to answer her phone for a several hours, both her lover and her brother rushed to her apartment and discovered that Faith had a high fever. She was in a coma. How could God let this happen? She was rushed to a hospital in New Orleans.

The Super Bowl was only two weeks away. Neither Rocky nor Thomas knew what to do. They cried and prayed together. Whenever Rocky or Thomas was at the hospital, Hope was also there, sitting quietly by Faith's side and holding her hand. Faith remained in a coma, and the days passed by. The doctors used many types of medication, the names of which no one could spell or pronounce. Nothing seemed to work, and Rocky couldn't help thinking that she would never recover. Surprisingly, Thomas became convinced during his isolated prayer sessions that Faith would soon recover and return to normal. Life, as he knew it, would resume. The days passed. Faith's status did not change, and the Super Bowl was getting closer. Both Thomas and Rocky realized it would be difficult to focus on the game. But it was only a game, and they both knew that sometimes there are more important things in life.

Two Quarterbacks Bite the Dust and Breakfast with Vince and Guido

O F UTMOST SIGNIFICANCE IS the fact that early on the morning of Super Bowl Sunday, when the sun rose, the Saints had three quarterbacks available for the game. This included their starting quarterback, Zoomer Washington. About six hours prior to the scheduled kickoff time, Jerry Yardley, the Saints' second-string quarterback, and Steve Sparrow, the Saints' third-string quarterback, were sharing a cab on the way to Sun Life Stadium. About five minutes into the ten-minute cab ride, a large truck cut off the taxi driver, who was forced to veer left into a concrete bridge abutment. Fortunately, the cab driver was not seriously injured. Unfortunately, Yardley suffered a dislocated kneecap, while Sparrow broke his left wrist and his right arm. Throughout the season, the Saints carried three quarterbacks. Both Yardley and Sparrow deserved to be on the Saints' roster. They both had numerous supporters who argued constantly that either one of them was good enough to be the starting quarterback on another team. Combined, they had thrown thirteen touchdown passes during the course of the season. In just moments, two of the Saints' three quarterbacks became unavailable for Super Bowl XLIV. Oh, my God! The Saints would play the game with only one quarterback. This was certainly not a super way to start "Super Sunday."

At precisely 8:00 a.m. on Super Bowl Sunday, Rudy Ruddast

met Vince and Guido at a diner near Sun Life Stadium for breakfast. Vince and Guido were almost perfect specimens of Italian men. They were both six feet three and had similar builds and the same wavy black hair, and they were both "tough guys." When they stood next to one another, they looked like a couple of Roman bookends. They were meeting because "they had things to discuss." After all, it was Super Bowl Sunday, and the three had figured out this was a day when Hope could make them rich.

Vince was the alpha Roman and looked as if he had spent just a little too much time eating pasta. He had a gravelly voice and always spoke softly. He walked into the diner with Guido and saw Rudy sitting on a bench in the waiting area. They both walked up to Rudy and said, "What's happening?" Vince added, "It's good to see that you made it. We weren't sure you would show up. And it's a good thing for you that you did show up. Right, Guido?"

Guido responded, "Yeah, boss! You said it would be best for Mr. Ruddast if he showed up." Guido spoke slower than most people and tried hard to enunciate every word. People who spent only a short period of time with Guido couldn't help thinking he didn't talk much and were convinced that he had a limited vocabulary.

The hostess seated the three men. Vince instructed the hostess, whose name was Jean, to tell their waitress that he wanted a "Number One" and Guido wanted a "Number Three." Both men requested coffee. Rudy indicated that he just wanted black coffee and wheat toast.

The hostess, coincidentally, was also Italian, and she boldly replied, "Yeah, yeah. Hold your horses! Who am I? Ya mother?" She went over and conversed noisily with one of the waitresses named Patty. Before the hostess relayed the breakfast orders, Patty volunteered that it was her opinion that the two Italian guys who had just sat down could have a contest to determine which one of them looked more Italian. She thought each one of them looked like he had just gotten off a boat from Italy and that either one of them could win the contest.

Rudy spoke to Vince and Guido. "You pasta-heads know why we're here. Yesterday, you had nothin'. Today, you're gonna get some Hope, and you're gonna get rich. Since I'm the brains, I get five hundred thousand, and Vince gets five hundred thousand, and he decides how he wants to split it. We are going to kidnap Hope and we're going to demand payment of one million dollars. It will be simple, and it will be sweet. And this is what we are going to do." He proceeded to provide more details to Vince and Guido, but he wasn't sure if Guido understood a single word he said. Rudy provided Vince with Hope's cell phone number and said he would meet up with him and Guido, as planned, after the game. About a half hour later, they paid their bill and left a generous tip for Patty, and Vince affectionately patted the hostess's lower back on the way out. Jean muttered something that sounded neither nice nor appreciative under her breath.

Radix omnium malorum est cupiditas. "The love of money is the root of all evil. Avarice is the problem, money itself is not evil."

Back at Sun Life Stadium and the Good, the Bad, and the Ugly

IT WAS LATE IN the afternoon, and a distinguished-looking elderly man with snow-white hair and wearing a New Orleans Saints jersey and cap sat in a lawn chair a few feet off the sidewalk, about a quarter mile away from the stadium. When he spotted a younger man walking purposefully down the sidewalk toward the stadium in the midst of a dense crowd of people, the older man yelled out, "J. C.! I'm over here!"

J. C. stopped in his tracks and exclaimed, "Father Joseph, what in the world are you doing here? I really didn't expect to see you today!"

Joe retorted, "I wouldn't miss this day for anything in the universe! I have to tell you that this game is causing great distress and anxiety for your mother."

J. C. explained, "We all know why I'm here today. This is something that just has to be done."

Joe nodded, "Your mother is here somewhere, and she just doesn't understand any of this. She is convinced that you should not play in this game."

J. C. shook his head and offered, "I am absolutely positive that she will find me."

Joe replied, "Yes, I'm sure she will. I just wanted to see you to wish you the best of luck." Joe stood up and extended his arm and fist and emphasized, "Go get 'em. Win one for the Gipper! For the most part, I haven't paid much attention to very many football games. Remember that Immaculate Reception in the Steelers game?"

With a pensive stare, J. C. simply replied, "Okay, Pops. I have to go!" With a sheepish grin, he walked towards the stadium.

The Virginia Villains were a formidable opponent. Their uniforms were black and blood red. Their jerseys, helmets, and pants were black, while each helmet and jersey had a nasty-looking red devil with fierce, bulging, bloodshot eyes. The devil had prominent horns protruding from its head, its body was engulfed in flames, and it possessed an ominous pointed tail. On Halloween, it was just about the best scary costume that anyone could wear.

The Villains were the good, the bad, and the ugly. They were good because they were gifted and talented athletes. They were bad because they possessed mean temperaments. They were ugly because of just one player, Henry Hershee, the Villains' nose tackle. In his mind, he felt that his position allowed him to move all over the field. Henry was one mean and nasty guy. His teammates concluded he was totally immune to pain. Perhaps he derived pleasure from the fact that, regardless of the pain he could endure, he could almost always inflict more pain upon someone else. Henry was a large man who looked like he had been chiseled out of granite. He was six feet five and weighed 285 pounds. Trying to determine the percentage of body fat on Henry would be an exercise in futility, as he just didn't have any. Henry's hairstyle was a buzz cut. He had all of his teeth except the two front ones. This look gave him an appearance that he was proud of. Therefore, the one thing Henry did not want for Christmas was his "two front teeth." He had a large disfigured nose that had been broken several times. If asked, Henry couldn't recall exactly how many times it had been broken. Whenever Henry made a tackle, he would typically cough, burp, scratch, belch, fart, and pull hair from an opponent's arms, legs, eyebrows, and nostrils. He boasted that he was the meanest and nastiest "mother" ever to sit on the Group W bench. There was a Group W bench in an old movie where Army recruiters directed prospective recruits to sit while they tried to determine if they were moral enough to kill women and children.

Henry Hershee was a nasty man. He was born to be a bully. He was a superbully who was playing in the Super Bowl. As an only child, he had been constantly abused verbally by his nasty grandmother, who had lived with his family. They had lived in the Midwest, but she was a dead ringer for the Wicked Witch of the West. During almost every conversation she ever had with Henry, she made it explicitly clear to him that he was stupid, ignorant, lazy, ugly, completely worthless, and that he would never amount "to a hill of beans." Henry's mother was an abused woman and lived her life in a closed and private world. She abused Henry by almost never talking to him or listening to him. She was always off in a corner minding her own business. She really didn't care what Henry did or didn't do. She didn't care about anything or anyone. For all of the interaction between them, she might as well have lived on a different planet. Henry's father, John Hershee, was an ill-tempered alcoholic who was drunk from the moment he crawled out of bed in the morning until he passed out at night. He beat Henry for good reasons and for no reasons at all. He abused Henry sexually. As a young teenager, Henry once pleaded for help from the school counselor, who quickly concluded that he could also sexually abuse the youngster whenever the father wasn't around. Henry was scarred for life.

Henry and his abusive family lived in Chicago. A few months after Henry turned thirteen, his grandmother died. A few months later, his mother suddenly got ill. The doctors could not identify a specific illness, and it wasn't long before she decided to die, for no apparent reason. Within a week, after administering just a few last beatings, Henry's father disappeared forever. Henry was raised in several foster homes. Needless to say, he moved frequently. Wherever he stayed he wasn't wanted.

Henry was born to be a bully. He put the "bull" in bully. None of the other bullies ever tried to bully Henry. Henry was always a big kid, and he grew into a man who was close to three hundred pounds of pure and simple meanness. Other kids did the best they could to stay away from him. The bull was never in Durham until Henry was about eight years old, and his parents took him on a quick trip for a family reunion to the Carolinas. When Henry was about ten years old, he was in a fine China shop with his mother for just a few minutes and suddenly, both his mother and the proprietor of the China shop concluded Henry should leave the store as soon as possible. Henry was the "bully" in a China shop.

Henry called himself "The Hershee Kiss." He would often kiss his right knuckles in front of another kid and then grab that kid's head with his left hand, pulling the unwilling head toward him and aggressively grinding the knuckles of his right hand into the person's forehead for a couple of seconds. Whenever Henry did this he would simply say, "Me kiss!" Being the recipient of a kiss from Henry was not a pleasant experience. On Saturday afternoons, if the kids knew Henry was on the north side of town, they would travel to the south side of the city to stay away from him. The neighborhood girls said whenever they saw Henry was nearby, they thought of a scenario where someone would place a chocolate kiss in their mouth but it would somehow have a large piece of aluminum foil with it which would instantaneously find a loose filling in the back of the mouth and painfully attack every isolated nerve ending in the body.

Henry strongly encouraged his Villains' teammates, especially the Farmer brothers, to hit their opponents and then to hit them again when they were down. Henry always wanted to apply the final "crunch" during a tackle. At the precise moment that he tackled someone, he would shout, "Me crunch!" He had acute hearing, and he loved to hear bones crackle when he tackled his opponents. Hershee claimed that whenever he made a tackle he could envision himself knocking down a concrete wall. In fact, one of the times he suffered a broken nose was when he literally attempted to knock over a concrete wall. It happened on a Saturday night a few years before the 2009–10 season, during the off-season. One of Hershee's associates dared him to try to knock over a concrete barrier; so Hershee gave it his best shot, face first. Just how mean and nasty was he? Hershee was so mean and nasty even his teammates didn't want to stand next to him in their defensive huddles.

The Villains had some other key players, including a linebacker named Jimmy Pillotti. He was only about half as mean as Henry, but he was still darn mean. The Villains' quarterback was Skippy Milano, and their fullback was Danny McCardle. In addition, there were the Farmer brothers, Mike and Mickey, who grew up on a farm in northern Minnesota. Like Pillotti, they were both defensive linebackers. Mike was born on a late Saturday afternoon in his parents' barn, after his mother slipped and fell while milking the cow. About a half hour later, Mike arrived in a makeshift bed of blankets and straw. Mickey was born almost a year later after his mother, who was working in the garden, had a sudden urge to go to the hospital. But she didn't make it. Mickey was born in the pickup truck on the way to the hospital. There were no other brothers or sisters.

Mike and Mickey always did chores from before dawn to dusk. As kids, they had to complete farm chores before and after school. They gathered eggs from the chickens, milked the cow, sheared the sheep, and planted and picked almost every vegetable and fruit known to mankind.

They were relentless and driven to master everything they ever encountered or thought about. They were industrious, hardworking, and clever. They constantly created games to play with the farm animals and livestock. They wrestled with the pigs, the baby calves, and the two sheep, a male and a female, which they cleverly named "Mr. Mike and Mickshelle." They constantly "teamed up." One would say, "You grab the cat and I'll get the rooster or one of the chickens, and then we'll throw the cat right on top of his fowl opponent." Then they would just explode with laughter at the barnyard ruckus. They would throw chicken eggs at the dogs. They would squirt milk from the cow at any creature that was within striking distance. They never really hurt the animals, but they figured that, since the animals were there, they might as well have a good time with them.

Around the farm, the brothers relentlessly pursued the rodents in the barn and the gophers in the fields. Therefore, it was fitting that they both became Minnesota Gophers after graduating high school. They both played the position of linebacker, where they could roam the field and try to hit everything that moved. Frequently, it was a brotherly act. One brother would hit or tackle a player on the other team, making sure to hit him "high," while the other brother inevitably was there at almost the same exact time to hit the opponent "low." They weren't dirty players; they were just both convinced that it was their job to put you on the ground and make sure you stayed there. They both thoroughly understood their roles on the team.

Henry Hershee was fond of the brothers. Mike and Mickey knew that a fight wasn't over until it was over, but they learned from Hershee that a football play wasn't necessarily over just because the whistle blew. They knew to hit hard, but he taught them to keep on hitting. He taught them that you hit a man on the way down and again after he's on the ground. They hit, they hit, and they hit again. Whenever Mike and Mickey stood near each other, Hershee would walk over to them and exclaim, "Me Like Farmers," in an attempt to manifest his appreciation of them.

J. C. and the Hot Dog

IT WAS APPROXIMATELY SIX o'clock in the evening, and the game was scheduled to begin at six thirty. J. C. stood quietly with folded hands as if he was in the midst of concentrated meditation. He stood on the sidewalk directly in front of Sun Life Stadium. He appeared to be talking to himself as he stared toward the upper levels of the stadium. If anyone had been watching, he or she might have noticed that a faint nimbus seemed to exist around the man's head and shoulders. As he continued having a quiet conversation with himself, he appeared to be oblivious to the world around him. Suddenly, he shouted like an excited chef, "Bam! It's time!" He picked up an empty candy wrapper off the ground and walked toward a female ticket taker named Karin. As he handed Karin the wrapper, she stared hypnotically into his eyes and smiled. Karin had just about the nicest smile in the entire universe. She let him into the stadium without even looking at his fabricated ticket, and he proceeded to the concessions area.

His olfactory senses kicked in. The distinct smells of hot dogs, popcorn, and cotton candy permeated the atmosphere. First, J. C. detected a whiff of a Polish sausage with onions and peppers. He thought about it but couldn't remember why this type of sausage was credited with having some kind of Polish ancestry. Then he noted a waft of buttery popcorn in the air, and he thought about how clever it was that corn or some form thereof went into just about anything you could think of. It could even be popped up to have a bag or bowl full of puffy delights. The intake and outtake fans created a wisp of air currents that brought in the distinct smells of peanuts and beer. A

29

fleeting thought occurred to J. C. that he just might have to sample the peanuts and beer when he had a chance. There was a whiff, a waft and a wisp. All the smells were distinct, but they somehow blended together deliciously. It was, in J. C.'s opinion, "olfactory heaven." He paused amidst the smells and bowed his head down toward the middle of his chest. As he lowered his chin, the disappearing sun flickered behind J. C. De Lord's head as it traversed its daily route toward another awesome Florida sunset. Surprisingly, only one person out of thousands in the busy crowd noticed the flickering sun. This person was a ten-year-old boy named Jimmy. He pointed toward the sky frantically and tugged on his mother's arm as he shouted, "Mom! Why is there so much light around that man's head?" Although the boy's mother was obviously involved in a dedicated conversation with another woman, she responded obediently to her son's question. She turned and focused briefly in the direction her son was pointing, towards the stranger. Her eyes returned rapidly to her son's bewildered face. For some unexplainable reason, she felt compelled to look in J. C.'s direction again, and after concentrating for several intense seconds, she concluded, "Jimmy, it just looks like he has a lot of light around his head because, after all, he's standing directly in front of the sunset."

After providing the boy with this logical explanation, in conjunction with fulfilling a maternal obligation, the woman turned to continue her conversation with the other woman. She snuck a furtive glance toward the sun and noticed the man was no longer standing there. She couldn't see where he went and once again refocused her attention to the other woman. Jimmy, however, maintained a pensive stare and watched the man intently. The man raised his head and immediately became aware of the boy staring at him, despite the tremendous amount of hustle and bustle in the area. The man smiled warmly, and his eyes sparkled with delight. The two were separated by no more than about ten feet. The boy stepped aggressively toward the stranger and boldly inquired, "Mister, who are you?"

J. C. hesitated momentarily and then responded in a noticeably self-assured manner, "Jimmy, today I guess I am an old quarterback who has been away for a long time. In fact, I guess I have been away for much too long!"

"How did you know my name is Jimmy?" asked the boy without any show of disbelief.

The stranger provided a logical explanation, "Your mother just spoke with you and called you Jimmy, didn't she?"

The youth nodded in agreement but would not relinquish the inquisitive expression that filled his cherubic, little face. Jimmy proceeded boldly with his interrogation, "Mister, are you really a football player?"

After just a brief moment of reflection, J. C. said, "I'm like George Washington; I cannot tell a lie. Let me just say that I have to get ready to play some football in the second half of today's game." He then asked Jimmy if he liked the game of football.

This question triggered a response from the boy as if he had just been plugged into an electrical socket. He enthusiastically offered, "I sure do, sir!" He stepped closer and added, "I really like the Saints a whole lot! My family and I used to live in New Orleans before Hurricane Katrina destroyed our home. The Saints are awesome!"

"Jimmy, I really like the Saints myself. I like all the Saints and people everywhere. I guess that's the reason I came to this game today. I'm sorry that you lost your house during the hurricane. Sometimes Mother Nature does things we don't understand, but I know you and your family will be okay. You just need to keep the faith. Jimmy, I'm certain that you are a very nice young man, and I really wouldn't be surprised if you become a Saint someday."

The boy's eyes widened and he exclaimed proudly, "I sure hope so, sir! I play football all the time with my older brother and my friends. I dream of playing football for the New Orleans Saints because my family misses Louisiana. Of course, I wouldn't mind playing for the Miami Dolphins either."

Jimmy was bright and perceptive enough to realize the man might be hungry. After all, the man was somewhat shabbily dressed, and he was wearing simple sandals with no socks. To Jimmy, this suggested the possibility that he might be hungry or thirsty. With these thoughts racing through his mind, Jimmy said, "I really like to play halfback, because I love to run with the ball! I wonder if that might be the best position for me to play. By the way, Mister, are you hungry? Would you like to share my hotdog?" The youth then proceeded to extract the remnants of a half-eaten hotdog from his rain jacket.

J. C. quickly provided the boy with a philosophical answer. "Jimmy, I want you to understand that it really does not matter what position we play in life. Every position we play and everything we do is important. And I appreciate your generous offer, but I really don't think that I should eat before a game. I also have to say that I think it was never anyone's intent that prime rib and hot dogs would come from the same animal. Jimmy, what's that by your foot? Well, Jesus Christ! Incidentally, I can say that and don't have to say excuse me." He grinned. "It's a twenty-dollar bill! It's not mine, and I really have no use for it. So here, you take it and keep it!" J. C. reached into a pocket and pulled out another twenty and handed both twenties to Jimmy, saying, "With only twenty bucks, you only would have had enough money to buy another hot dog and a bottle of water."

The previously talkative young man became speechless but just as quickly regained his composure and repeated the same question he had asked several minutes earlier, "Mister, who are you?"

"Jimmy, you can call me J. C. I really have to get to the Saints' locker room, but I have a feeling that we will probably meet again someday in the distant future. Take care of yourself, and take care of your mother. She is a very special person." Without any further discussion, he turned and disappeared into the crowd.

The boy looked down at his hands, and when he looked up, J. C. was gone. Jimmy softly said, "Good-bye. Thanks for everything!" He raced over to his mother's side and once again tugged on her arm in an attempt to distract her from the relentless conversation with the other woman. He wanted to tell her immediately about his conversation and how his new friend, J. C., was going to play in the game. Sometimes mothers think that their children are annoying and aggravating. Sometimes they think they would like to be far away from their kids on extended vacations. But, when mothers sit down and think about it and put everything into perspective, they always want to be right there with their children. Jimmy continued to pull on his mother's arm, but she did not look at him.

What Is a Quarterback?

J. C. WALKED TOWARD the Saints' locker room and understood he would be playing the position of quarterback for the Saints during the second half of the game. What is a quarterback? Generically, a quarterback, in the game of football, is a leader, a director, a commander. There are numerous words that define a quarterback, but not a single word seems to be adequate by itself. A quarterback is a guide, a conductor, a pilot, a captain, a chief, a commander, an engineer, a president, an authoritative figure, a figurehead, a spokesperson, a helmsman, a starter, a premier, a dictator, a chairman, a superintendent, a chauffeur, and a guiding star (perhaps the North Star). In sports, there are captains, cocaptains, pacers, players who set the pace, centers, centers of attention, point guards, guards who seem to guard no one and get paid a lot of money to do this, field engineers, clean-up hitters, number-one seeds, masters, goaltenders, and anchormen. In the game of football, a quarterback possesses a combination of these traits, characteristics, and responsibilities. However, a quarterback has followers and disciples. A quarterback, like other leaders, is often the man who is primarily responsible for leading his team to either victory or defeat. Finally, many of us might agree that a quarterback may possess incredible abilities, but his chances of becoming a gridiron star are limited unless he has the respect and support of his followers and teammates. The quarterback is the key figure. It is very difficult to win a football game without a talented and proficient quarterback.

John 11:16: Thomas said, "Let us also go, that we may die with him."

The Game and a Kidnapping

THE GAME HAD ONLY been in progress for about three minutes and the Villains had just scored their first touchdown when Hope Evig's cell phone rang in the owner's box, which was filled with at least a dozen people, including her mother and father. Hope answered the phone as she watched the extra point attempt travel into the net after its successful passage between the goalposts. She didn't recognize the number that came up on her phone and wondered who it could be. She answered and said, "Hello."

An unfamiliar voice at the other end identified himself as "Tony" at the hospital. Hope immediately remembered that Tony was one of the nurses who provided loving care to Faith at the hospital twenty-four hours a day. There was a lot of noise in the owner's suite, and Hope requested, "Please hold for just a second while I step out of the room." She had recently spent a lot of time at the hospital, and she thought that the voice didn't really sound like Tony's voice. As she stepped out of the room and took several steps down a hallway, the voice related, "Miss Evig, I am sorry to report that there is bad news concerning Faith. She has taken a turn for the worse, and the doctors believe the end might be near. Two men will be there in just a few seconds to escort you to a special phone where you will be able to speak with her primary physician."

Hope sighed, stood still, and said mechanically, "Okay, good-bye."

As soon as Hope exited the suite, Vince moved towards the same door and handed a white envelope to a bubbly waitress named

34

Joyce, who was entering the suite with a tray full of appetizers. He also gave her a ten-dollar bill and commanded, "Sweetheart, please deliver this to Mr. Charles Evig, the owner of the Saints, and don't give it to anyone else!"

It appeared that the girl hardly noticed him—she was too busy chewing bubblegum and trying to balance her tray. She nodded, "Okay, honey. You betcha!" Vince was wearing white gloves when he handed her the envelope and removed them immediately after she took it from him. After he relinquished the envelope, he took a few steps toward Hope and placed his hand on her shoulder while Guido approached her from the opposite direction and placed his hand on her other shoulder.

Obediently, the waitress entered the suite and delivered the envelope directly to Mr. Evig, stammering, "It's for you sir!" Mr. Evig was somewhat stout in stature and of average height, and he had thinning gray hair. He was seated near a large glass window that provided him with a bird's-eye view of the field. As the waitress handed him the envelope, a bald eagle appeared directly in front of the window, just a few feet away. The eagle flew in front of him and looked directly into his eyes. Mr. Evig understood the eagle's presence was foreboding. The eagle had a distinctive white head, and his tail feathers indicated he was mature and at least four or five years old. His majestic wingspan was approximately seven feet.

Mr. Evig was doing his best to cope with the touchdown that had just been scored by the Villains. He muttered numerous obscenities as he took possession of the envelope in a somewhat tentative manner and the eagle flew away out of sight. When he secured the envelope in his hands, he immediately tore into it in a businesslike manner and removed one piece of bond paper with a typewritten note that read:

THIS IS A RANSOM NOTE!!

We have taken your daughter Hope. We are not greedy, and we also understand this is a Sunday and you will not be able to transact any business with a bank. We only want one million dollars.

We want it delivered to us in four New Orleans Saints' duffel bags with $250k in each one.

We want you to procure a total of one hundred and four duffel bags from the concession stands. We want one hundred of the duffel bags delivered to us with only paper in them. You will deliver four of the paper-filled duffel bags to twenty-five locations, and we will tell you where to deliver the four bags filled with money.

We have calculated that the average person will spend $29 at the game today. If you multiply that by fifty or sixty thousand people, that's well over a million dollars. Mr. Evig, the money is at your fingertips. You don't have to go to any bank. This is a quick and dirty deal!

You have until the second-half kickoff to deliver the money. If you are not ready to deliver it, then you better make sure that the football is not kicked off until you deliver the money.

Don't tell the authorities. Just deliver the money!

If you don't, Hope might get hurt or die!
Imagine that, life without Hope!
We will provide more details in the very near future.

The blood drained from Charles Evig's face, and he exclaimed to those around him, "Oh God! Please help me!" He handed the note to his wife, Sophia, who was seated right next to him.

Sophia was dressed from head to toe as if she were attending the Kentucky Derby. A woman just couldn't look any better than she did. As she began to read the note, her eyebrows almost came off the top of her forehead. Sophia was a woman who was used to taking charge. She gasped for air and shouted, "Charlie, let's pull ourselves together and start gathering all of the duffel bags. We both know that we are not going to debate this or try to negotiate with these hoodlums. We're going to give them the money as soon as possible. Hope is so precious. She really is a good girl, and she means the world to both of us. I will take responsibility for gathering the required number of bags, 104, I believe. Charles, you will take responsibility for collecting the money, which will be divided and then deposited into four of the bags!" Before Charlie could even utter a word, Sophia continued, "I just had a thought. We are going to get all of the Saints' cheerleaders to help us gather the duffel bags and stuff one hundred of them with paper. Of course, you realize that I know each and every one of those sweet darlings and they would be willing to do anything to help us out. In fact, I just decided that the Villains' cheerleaders are also going to help us out. I am leaving to gather all of the girls together, and we will have all 104 duffel bags delivered back to this location in about thirty minutes. The bottom line is that all of the bags will definitely be ready for the kidnappers in about an hour."

Charles nodded his head authoritatively and said, "So far, Sophia, I totally agree with you. Let's go!" He reached for the telephone to contact the head of security and the stadium's concessions manager. Sophia immediately left the room to gather the cheerleaders and guide them on a life or death mission.

Just a few minutes later, the fans noticed all of the Saints' cheerleaders and all of the Villains' cheerleaders mingling together. Then, suddenly, they all raced off the field, with a meaningful purpose.

Meanwhile, Vince and Guido still had their hands on Hope's shoulders, and before she even realized it, they were escorting her away as Vince politely demanded, "Miss Evig, please come with us!"

Hope cried and cooperated fully for the first thirty seconds as they walked down a hallway, but then she attempted to pull her arms away and demanded, "Who are you guys? You don't have anything to do with the hospital. Why are you being so rough with me?" Tears rolled down her cheeks.

Guido replied, "Listen, babe. You're coming with us and you ain't got no choice in the matter. Besides, I've seen both girls and guys cry before. It doesn't matter to me!"

Hope insisted, "You can't take me away like this. There are security people all over this place."

Vince explained, "Miss Hope, we have guns in our pockets.

We are in the process of kidnapping you, and we will both shoot you dead in a heartbeat if you don't cooperate and come with us peacefully." The men continued to escort her gently down the hall. Hope did not manifest any noticeable emotion as she was doing her best to get herself under control to deal with the situation at hand. Vince explained, "We are going to take you away, and then we're going to give you back as soon as your father, Mr. Evig, gives us a lot of money."

Guido concurred by adding, "Yeah! That's what's gonna happen."

While they were walking, they encountered a waitress, a maintenance man wearing headphones and listening to some god-awful music, and three teenage girls who were walking together but all having individual conversations on their cell phones. One of the girls spoke louder than the other two, and Vince, Guido, and Hope heard her say, "Susie called Mary and then she told Sally that Jennifer said she didn't like my new outfit but she really thought that Christine's new outfit was really cute." Coincidentally, the only other person they passed was J. C. Guido led the way, followed by Hope, who was nudged along by Vince. As they turned around a corner Vince looked back at Hope and walked directly into J. C. Vince looked at J. C. and barked, "Oh God, please watch where you're goin'!"

J. C. glanced at them and replied, "I believe I know where *you* are going." Hope looked at J. C. in a covert manner and mouthed *help me*. J. C. winked emphatically at Hope and kept walking toward his destination, the Saints' locker room. Hope noticed the stranger's wink and felt comforted by it despite the fact that the man kept walking away from them.

Guido shrugged his shoulders, grabbed Hope's left hand, and said, "C'mon, let's go!" They walked down another nearby hallway and turned right. Their entire journey lasted only a couple of hundred feet, and then they arrived at a door labeled "Utility Room." Guido unlocked it with a key, and the two kidnappers and their hostage entered the room and closed the door. Inside the room there were three chairs and about ten bottles of water.

Meanwhile, a couple of dozen cheerleaders were scattered all over the concession area. They were running in every conceivable direction as they frantically procured duffel bags and stuffed them with any kind of paper they could find, including newspapers, napkins, paper towels, hot dog wrappers, and paper cups. Mrs. Evig quickly selected four pairs of girls to gather the ransom money from the concession stands, cash registers, and safes. Of course, as the girls were still wearing their skimpy cheerleader outfits, they attracted a lot of attention as they jiggled and bounced their way through the concourse areas.

After Vince, Guido, and Hope entered the utility room, Vince offered Hope a metal folding chair to sit on and handed her a bottle of water. "You can see that I am really a true gentleman," he said.

Hope gathered her thoughts and blasted out, "How dare you take advantage of a situation where my best friend is in a coma? You tricked me and kidnapped me. You should be ashamed of yourselves! What you are doing is utterly despicable!"

Vince replied, "Yeah, it's despicable, but we're gonna get rich in about an hour. We got a good plan! Guido has arranged for some of his friends to hand out dozens of duffel bags randomly to people throughout the stadium. It's going to create a diversion while Guido and I escape with the four duffel bags filled with money. It's a good plan, and it can't go wrong!"

Guido asked, "Hey, Vince, what's a diversion?"

Hope said, "You guys are despicable idiots."

Zoomer Becomes
a Sandwich

OF COURSE, THE VIRGINIA Villains were a good, solid football team. They had finished the regular season with fourteen wins and two losses. Then they were victorious over the Denver Broncos and the New York Jets on their way to the Super Bowl.

The first half of the game was almost over, and it had been relatively entertaining, especially if you were a Villains' fan. In fact, it had been a lopsided affair. Actually, it was an absolutely horrendous half of football for the Saints. It just couldn't get any worse. There was slightly less than a minute remaining in the half, and the Villains were leading the Saints by a score of forty-two to three. It seemed as if the Saints had played the first half without any emotional conviction. All over the world, hands were reaching for remotes and fingers were changing channels.

During the half, the Villains had scored six touchdowns with several time-consuming drives. They converted all six of their extra point attempts. Their first score came after a twenty-one-yard touchdown reception about three minutes into the game. Their second score followed an interception and an amazing sixty-two-yard pass on the following possession. The football bounced off a defender's helmet and then went directly into the hands of one of the Villains' wide receivers. They proceeded to take a twenty-one-point lead on an eight-yard run up the middle on the second play of the second quarter. Shortly thereafter, the Saints finally got on the scoreboard after a promising drive fizzled and their placekicker, Brian Jode, split the crossbars with a twenty-eight-yard field goal to make the score twenty-one to three. This meager field goal did not slow down the charge of the powerful Villains. Within the next five minutes, the Villains scored three additional touchdowns: one on an eighteen-yard crossing pattern, one on a fourteen-yard down-and-out pattern, and one on a one-yard dive over the left tackle with just under a minute to play in the half.

The Saints and their fans thought it just couldn't get any worse. With only forty-six seconds remaining in the first half, J. C. was inside the stadium, and he momentarily took an unoccupied seat at the end of an aisle, approximately forty rows up from the playing field, near the fifty-yard line. He understood that he still had plenty of time.

The Saints' quarterback, Zoomer Washington, had just completed a twelve-yard pass to his tight end, Andrews, who was tackled on the Saints' forty-eight-yard line. After the tackle, Zoomer called a time-out, which left the Saints with only one more time-out in the half. Zoomer (whose real name was Melvin) was a brash and flashy guy. He was a bold, brazen, smooth talker who was full of himself. He was a talented quarterback, and he had long, flowing hair. He had the kind of locks that most women would trade three or four pairs of shoes and a couple of pocketbooks to have as their own.

J. C. quietly and intently watched the Saints huddle. They broke from the huddle and approached the line of scrimmage for their next play. It was first down. Zoomer took the snap, and within just a couple of short ticks of the clock, he threw an incomplete pass just beyond the outstretched hands of Andrews, about eight yards downfield, next to the far sideline. A woman who was sitting directly behind J. C. yelled, "Oh God!" For some reason, J. C. just turned around and looked at her inquisitively, but he didn't say anything. The situation was obviously a critical one for the Saints. They had to score some points before the half ended to get themselves into a position where they could still overcome the apparently insurmountable deficit of forty-two to three.

As the Saints returned to the huddle to prepare for their second-down play, J. C. stood up and purposely walked through the same exit he had just entered a few minutes earlier. He walked up the aisle without ever looking back at the playing field, and he was gone.

Zoomer took the snap in a shotgun formation. (The Saints' owners probably should have used a shotgun on the entire team for the way they played in the first half.)

It was a pass play. The Villains' linebackers, the Farmer brothers, came on a blitz. The brothers came charging full-speed towards Zoomer from opposite directions. Zoomer never knew what hit him. It was as if he were a stationary piece of roasted turkey captured between two giant pieces of rye bread that had slipped in from different directions in a concerted effort to make a Super Bowl sandwich. As Zoomer released the pass and was falling to the ground, the nose tackle, Hershee, came in for the final kiss. Hershee hit Zoomer viciously, helmet first, in the back of his right knee, at the same time that one Farmer tackled high and one Farmer tackled low. While in midair, Zoomer's body made a valiant effort to contort in two antithetical directions. Zoomer's wide receiver, Willie Simon, caught the ball and raced to the Villains' fourteen-yard line before he was forced out of bounds. Incidentally, Willie Simon was by far the most talkative player on the team. He was smooth and glib, and he fancied the ladies. He chattered incessantly and would always say, "Give me the ball. I want the ball. I always want the ball."

The game clock stopped, and it seemed as if time itself had done the same. The Saints had a first down with thirty-four seconds remaining in the half. Zoomer could not and did not get up. He had been tackled simultaneously by three players, and nearby fans were convinced they heard three distinctive sounds: a snap, a crackle, and a pop ... and the noises had nothing to do with a bowl of cereal. Zoomer was down, and he was hurt. Thousands of screaming fans suddenly went silent. It was incomprehensible how so many thousands of fans could make so little noise. It was the sound of concern mixed with the sound of silence. The chief referee, Billy Ives, the field judge, Ron Bishop, and the line judge, David Elder, cleared the space around Zoomer and gathered around him.

As Zoomer lay on the ground, writhing in pain, it was obvious to all that he was done for the day. His left leg had multiple fractures to both the fibula and the tibia. The replay on the stadium's wide screen showed that Zoomer's left leg had moved in completely unnatural ways during the tackle. Zoomer reacted to his injury like a real man should: he cried. He didn't cry because of the pain, but because he was so disappointed that he could no longer participate in the game, which meant so much to him. While the trainers and medical personnel attended to him during the next twenty minutes, it was quiet enough to hear a pin drop. An ambulance finally backed onto the field, and Zoomer was transported to the nearest hospital.

J. C. thought about Zoomer and said a prayer for him, "He who sees in me all things, and all things in me, is never far from me, and I am never far from him" (*The Bhagavad Gita*).

The Saints' coaching staff was stunned and didn't have any immediate ideas. Zoomer was out of the game, and the Saints did not have another quarterback in uniform. They had lost three quarterbacks in the same day. A quarterback is hard to find. Quarterbacks don't grow on trees like high-level executives, CEOs, and politicians. While Zoomer was sprawled on the ground, the team's offensive coordinator asked around and discovered that Dave Andrews, the tight end, had played backup quarterback in high school about eight years earlier. After Zoomer was taken from the field, the coaching staff certainly did not want to do anything stupid with just a few seconds left in the first half. Therefore, Andrews was put in the game, and he was directed to take the snap and hand the ball off to Rocky, the fullback, who ran straight towards the end zone, gaining about four yards before he was tackled. At this point, the game clock still had about thirty seconds on it, but every Saint was in a daze, and as they wandered around aimlessly, the time on the clock expired before they could attempt another play. They couldn't even figure out how to get back into a huddle. The Saints' organization and everyone everywhere were in shock. How could this possibly happen? Earlier that morning the Saints were reasonably optimistic that they could win this game. Now, there was no way on God's green Earth that they could even dream of being competitive in the second half of the game. The Saints' fans realized it was useless to even fantasize about winning this game. In fact, computer nerds were beginning to use sophisticated calculators to predict the final score, and within minutes, Vegas was projecting a final score of ninety-eight to three.

The Villains charged off the field with jubilant gestures and bloodcurdling screams of exultation. It was crystal clear to them and to the rest of the world that this Super Bowl was all but over! The game belonged to the Villains! The Saints morosely left the field as if they were taking part in a funeral procession. In fact, a band played the Dixieland Funeral March from the James Bond movie, "*Live and Let Die.*" The Saints realized they were at the end of their rope and the noose was tightening rapidly. As the Saints went down the tunnel towards their locker room, a number of security guards were directed to make certain that none of the media or any other unauthorized visitors entered the Saints' locker room during halftime.

For all practical purposes, the game was over. Several thousand fans filed mechanically from the stadium. They were hopeful that there might be better Super Bowl games in the future. Several hundred thousand television sets were either turned off or switched to other channels. The network personnel were frantic. How could anyone be interested in either watching or participating in the second half of this game? There would be no miracles!

But there were some who understood that the game ain't over until the fat lady sings. Anything can happen in love, war, and football games.

The Reporter, a Prediction, and Motherly Advice

URING THE SOMEWHAT EXTENDED period that Zoomer was on the ground and being treated by medical personnel, J. C. walked down a hallway that led to the Saints' locker room within the inner recesses of the stadium. J. C. turned a corner, and a young Hispanic woman who wasn't paying any attention to where she was going bumped into him. She began to apologize profusely. She went on and on without taking a breath about how sorry she was for having caused the collision. She said it was completely her fault. She was in her midtwenties. She was five feet two and was what many considered to be a "looker." Although she spoke English extremely well, she spoke it with an accent, and it was obvious she had descended from Spanish ancestry.

J. C. extended both of his hands toward her and said, "Excuse me, Miss Rivera! It's very nice to see you. I am truly very sorry, but I have to go suit up for the game."

She replied, "Sir, who are you, and what in the world are you talking about? And how do you know who I am?"

J. C. grinned and said, "Please, wait just a minute. You are asking way too many questions all at the same time. Of course, I know who you are. Everyone in south Florida knows who you are. You're the lady sportswriter who works for the *Miami Sunday Reporter*. Your name is Veronica Rivera."

Veronica responded, "Yes, that's correct, but ..."

The man on a mission volunteered proudly, "My name is De Lord. J. C. De Lord. I am thirty-three years old and I'm here for the Saints, who are in dire need of some help. As you know, it appears that they do not currently have a quarterback for the second half of today's game. Hopefully, I will be the answer to their prayers. You know, sometimes even the Saints can use some special help. I think it's about time the New Orleans Saints get more recognition in this world, and I'm here to help them accomplish that. You are the first newsperson I've told this to. I am going to play quarterback for the Saints today, and I am going to help them win the Super Bowl. Please excuse me, Miss Rivera, but I have to get going now."

Veronica scoffed, "Mr. De Lord, are you some kind of nut? Who are you? I've never heard of you, and I have been following the Saints all season. Just because you might have played some football in college or high school once upon a time doesn't mean that you can just stroll into the Saints' locker room and tell them that you want to be their quarterback. Also, my friends call me Ronnie. Please call me Ronnie." Without hesitation, she added, "The Saints are in dire straits. What makes you think that you can possibly save the Saints?"

J. C. replied, "I know I can. Ronnie, please listen carefully to what I am going to tell you. I never played football before. My old man likes football, and he and I have thrown the ball around. Once upon a time, many years ago, people thought I was a radical thinker. I had long hair and a beard, and I wore ragged clothing. I tried carpentry, and then I became, well, a fisherman. Nonetheless, I did what had to be done. People everywhere have to realize that we sometimes have to take aggressive action to stand up for what we believe in. You are a reporter. Now you're a reporter with a scoop. Get ready for a wild second half of football. Call your newspaper as soon as you can and tell them to hold the front page. In fact, I'm going to go out on a limb and predict the future. When the eagle soars, the Saints will win! Later, Miss Ronnie!" J. C. winked at her with sparkling blue eyes and spun around like a Radio City Music Hall Rockette. He walked briskly around the corner and proceeded down the hallway.

Ronnie stood there, her disbelief etched on her face. Within a few seconds, she regained her composure and stepped around the corner, but J. C. was nowhere to be seen. She whispered loudly, "Mr. De

Lord, who are you?" She fumbled around in her pocketbook, removed her cell phone, and scurried away in the other direction. She didn't know why, but she felt deep down within her soul that the second half would surely be a good one.

J. C. continued toward the Saints' locker room. He rounded another corner and exclaimed, "Holy Moses! Mother! What in heaven's name are you doing here?"

A refined matronly woman put her hands up to stop J. C. in his tracks. The woman looked to be around fifty, and she rebuked, "I'm here because I care about you. A mother should always be able to see her son. I was looking for you, and I couldn't find you. This reminds me of the time many years ago when you disappeared and I finally found you down at the market. Early this morning I couldn't find you, and when I asked where you were, your father was quite evasive. Finally, he told me where you were. He wasn't going to tell me, but I convinced him that he should or he might not get any dinner. He told me that you recently decided that you might play in some kind of Super Game of football which, incidentally, is a game that I am not fond of. What in the world are you doing here?" His mother's first name was Mary, and she possessed the most beautiful complexion. She had wide, roundish eyes that always seemed to be dilated just a smidgen more than most eyes. In fact, she had eyes like a lot of mothers, and they helped her see almost anything and everything happening around her.

"Oh, Mother! It's just a game. Actually, it's not just a game. It's the Super Bowl. It's the game where the two best football teams play a championship game."

"So, Son, how does this concern you? I believe I saw some football played before. You never played. Grown men run into each other and knock each other down. I think they try to score some points somehow. You should not play in this game. You might get hurt!"

"Mom, listen, I won't get hurt. I promised Father that I would be very careful today with respect to who gets hurt and who doesn't."

"I don't want you playing. It looks like a rough game to me, and it's been a very long time since you attempted to do anything like this."

"Mom, Father and I discussed this, and I have to play with some of the Saints."

Mary had a regal appearance with a slight trace of gray hair. She was an articulate woman. She was wearing a simple blue frock with plain leather sandals. She wore no makeup, as she never did. She wore no jewelry except for an amber necklace. She had no watch, no pocketbook, and no cell phone. She continued, "I saw some football players a little while ago, but I didn't see any saints. Why is it that no one ever tells me what's going on? I just don't understand why you have to play in some football game. Are there any saints here? I haven't seen any of them walking around. I just don't want you to play in the Super Bowl. If anyone tries to hurt you, I promise that I will take them aside and speak with them immediately."

"Mother, we just didn't want to give you any reason to be worried. You know there have been times in the past when I had to do certain things that you didn't necessarily approve of. This is one of those times. This is really a simple issue. I will play some football. The Saints will win the Super Bowl tonight, and then I'll be home later."

"Okay, then. I'm sure you will. But if you get hurt, don't say I didn't tell you so. I just think you shouldn't play. There really is no need for you to play, because the team you want to win could probably win anyway without your direct intervention."

"Mother, I really don't have time to discuss this any further with you. Later!" He hugged his mother and took a step away from her. He waved, smiled, turned, and walked down the hall with a purpose in his step.

Mary just stood there with a concerned expression and said to no one, "Later! Later than what? What does he mean when he just says 'later' to me and walks away?"

The Locker Room

WHEN THE FIRST HALF ended, the Saints and their coaching staff filed into their locker room as the halftime festivities began on the playing field. As always, the halftime show was set up to be spectacular! Hopefully, God wouldn't tolerate any wardrobe malfunctions. The players and coaches entered the locker room and gathered together with very little discussion or commotion. On the way to the locker room, the Saints' coach, Doc "Fumble" Pitts, was taken aside by a security officer and escorted into an office where Mr. Evig informed him of Hope's kidnapping, the ransom note, and the demand for one million dollars. Pitts understood that the second half would not begin until the ransom money was delivered.

Coach Pitts was one of the last people to enter the locker room before the door was slammed shut. As a collegiate player, Doc Pitts recovered an incredible number of fumbles, and this earned him the nickname of "Fumble." Usually, any reference to the word fumble has a negative connotation. This wasn't the case with Doc. "Fumble" was a nickname he was proud of. With hustle and a lot of hard work and a little bit of luck, he had earned that nickname. He was a great coach. He was adored and respected by everyone: the players, the fans, other coaches, and even the media. Fumble entered the locker room, forlorn and speechless. He possessed wavy golden hair, the kind of hair made for television commercials. He moved toward the center of the room and bewailed to his surrounding coaching staff, "Jimmy, Jerry, Neal, Randy! I have never experienced anything like this during my entire thirty years of coaching football. Over the past eight hours, we have somehow lost all three of our quarterbacks. We all know that a football game cannot be played without a quarterback. Who in the Sam Hill is going to play quarterback? I know this has never happened before to us or to any other team! Maybe we should just give up and go home. Maybe we should just forfeit by refusing to go back out onto the field. That might be a better choice than getting humiliated in front of a national television audience. Usually, in the Super Bowl blowouts in the past, people have stopped watching or have turned to other channels. I believe that might not happen this year. People everywhere will hang in there until the final whistle to watch the Saints lose by a score of a zillion to three. What are we going to do? God only knows who is going to play quarterback for us."

A man wearing a crisp, clean Saints' uniform with the number seven on it appeared from around a nearby locker and walked boldly toward the center of the room and announced clearly, "Coach Pitts, I just heard what you said. As you can see, I am holding a football in my hands. My name is De Lord. J. C. De Lord." He proceeded to announce emphatically, "I will be your quarterback in the second half of today's game."

Not unexpectedly, Pitts bellowed, "Who the hell are you and how did you get into our locker room and where did you get that uniform? It almost looks like one of ours."

Sam "Way Too Big" Sprigs, a second-string jumbo-sized offensive tackle, jumped up from a nearby bench and demanded, "Let me throw this crazy SOB out into the hallway, or better yet, I'll escort him to the closest parking lot and rearrange his body parts."

J. C. stood there in a brazen and confident manner. "Please, wait one moment! I truly understand that most of you will find this difficult to believe, but I'm here to help you win the Super Bowl. Face the facts! Your team does not have a quarterback for the remainder of this game. You lost three quarterbacks today! I have been preparing for this day for a long time. Without me, the Saints don't stand a chance of being competitive. I'm the only one in the universe who can help you win this game!"

Sprigs pleaded, "My God! I could take care of this in just a couple of minutes."

J. C. replied assuredly, "Please listen! God is not going to let you do that to me."

Everyone in the locker room was discussing the situation. Rocky, the fullback, blurted, "I don't know what's going on here, but I think we should hear him out." Virtually all of the chatter and noise subsided, and everyone turned his attention to the head coach.

Coach Pitts, in an extremely exasperated manner, cried, "I really don't have the time for this kind of horse hockey! Who are you?"

J. C. explained, "As I already told you, my name is J. C. De Lord. And as you can see, I have a Saints uniform with my name on it." J. C. turned around, and the name on the back of the uniform was indeed "J. C. De Lord." J. C. added, "I have a football and I have a uniform. And I am ready to play some football."

Coach Pitts demanded, "What in the Sam Hill do you know about football?"

J. C. smiled sardonically, "Coach Pitts, you might as well say I created the pigskin. I know everything I need to know, and I'll prove it to you!" One of the players had left his helmet near the water cooler, about a hundred feet from where J. C. was standing. J. C. announced, "See that helmet over there!" Then, using his right arm, he nonchalantly raised the football near his chin, spun toward the water cooler, and whipped a perfect spiral pass that wedged itself into a small opening in the helmet. The helmet moved back against the wall and remained motionless. There were "oohs" and "aahs" all around.

Pitts, who had been standing, sat down abruptly in total amazement and queried, "Mr. De Lord, where did you play football? Obviously, you've played some football somewhere."

J. C responded, "I have never played football before." In a split second, J. C. picked up another football with his left hand and threw it forcefully in an underhanded manner toward another helmet that was sitting on a bench just a couple of yards to the right of the same water cooler. This football, like the last one, lodged itself in the face of the open helmet. The helmet bounced off a locker and landed in a pile of towels.

Sprigs jumped to his feet and expostulated, "Amen!" With his eyes wide open he looked up and down and back and forth. He blessed himself rapidly and then sat back down as quickly as he could.

Coach Pitts experienced an instantaneous metamorphosis. His facial expression was similar to that of a young child in a candy store. "Mr. De Lord, I really don't know who you are, and I really don't care. I don't know what's happening, but I suddenly feel like I have a tremendous amount of faith in you, Mr. De Lord. May I call you J. C.?"

J. C. replied, "Of course you can. J. C.'s my name, and football is my game! I'm your man. Believe me! You really have to believe me when I say that if I can't do it, nobody can!"

Jerry Palmer, one of the assistant coaches, shared his disbelief, "So he either just got lucky or he can really throw a football extremely well at inanimate objects. He doesn't know any of our plays!"

J. C. replied, "Sir, I'm going to have to contradict what you just said. I know all of your plays. It's not important to explain why I know them, I just know them. Maybe I found one of your old playbooks in a trash barrel. For example, 'Star Three' is a passing play where the tight end, Dave Andrews, lines up next to the right tackle. The left end, Tommy Allmen, splits left while the halfback, Hay Jude, lines up a couple of yards closer to the line, and the right end, Willie Simon, goes in motion and cuts in back of the line to the left side of the field. After the ball is hiked, Thomas runs a wide out pattern, Simon goes long on a down-and-out route, and Jude goes down across the middle from left to right. Andrews delays about a count and a half, then goes straight down the field four or five yards and turns around for a buttonhook pass in the middle of the field. Ask me a play, any play!"

Pitts, somewhere between a stupor and complete euphoria, shouted out, "Thirty-four Z!"

J. C., without a moment of hesitation, explained, "The quarterback, namely me, takes the snap, fakes a handoff to the running back, Jude, who will run to the outside without the ball, after which I'll give the ball to the fullback, Rocky, who will take it directly through the four hole! We're wasting time. Let's go out there and play some football!"

At this point, Thomas, the left end, entered the room for the first time since J. C. arrived. He had been in the bathroom. He looked directly at Coach Pitts and asked, "What's going on here?"

Pitts explained, "I don't really know what's going on here. We might be looking at the Saints' only chance to win this game. We were desperate, and now there might be hope!"

J. C. suggested, "I would like to say that in a slightly different way. First there was darkness, but now there is light!"

Thomas quipped, "Well, I don't know if I believe this. What's going on here?"

J. C. responded authoritatively, "I'm not surprised that you don't believe in me."

Rocky rebuked, "Hey, pal, we don't even know you. Why don't you just leave us alone and get out of here before some of our linemen rearrange your pretty face!"

J. C. pointed out, "You said you don't know me. Look. There's a program for today's game lying on the bench over there. Pick it up and look at the official roster on page four. There you will see my name, next to the number seven."

Thomas replied sarcastically, "Sure, you're on the Saints' roster, and my name is Cinderella."

Andrews grabbed the official program to put an end to this nonsense. He flipped quickly to page four. He studied the roster for a few seconds and then handed it to Thomas, relating, "Yes, his name is listed in the program. I don't understand. Quick, look at another program!"

Several players frantically grabbed for other programs. Within seconds, they were holding up the programs and shouting out that De Lord's name was, in fact, listed there.

Sprigs exclaimed, "Holy Moses! Your name really is on the roster. How did that happen? Who are you, man? Who are you?"

J. C. explained, "We're not talking about Moses here. We're talking about me."

Michael McHale, the equipment manager, bolted toward the center of the room and blurted out, "I've been this team's equipment manager for six years. Nothing like this has ever happened to me before. Last week, I was performing an inventory of the equipment, and I discovered a uniform with the name De Lord on it. I realized that the number seven hadn't been used by any of our players all season. I thought that someone was trying to play some kind of joke on me. After a couple of days passed and no one said anything to me about the uniform, I just tossed it into an empty locker. I also have to tell you that I saw De Lord's name on a computer printout a few days ago. The printout indicated he was a quarterback, but no other pertinent information was available. To be honest, neither myself nor any of my assistants ever heard of him before, so we just didn't pay much attention when a uniform with his name on it appeared. We were busy preparing for today's game, and we didn't think it was worth mentioning any of this to anyone else. As far as his uniform is concerned, I never ordered it, and I don't know where it came from. Every player received a brand new uniform for this game. His uniform looks just as authentic as all of the other uniforms."

Pitts redirected a question he had previously asked, "Who is this man and where did he come from?" He was looking up at the ceiling as he said this and wasn't really asking anyone in particular.

In a complacent manner, J. C. volunteered, "I have already told you, this will be one of those things that happens during your lifetime that you might have difficulty understanding. The Saints' organization has absolutely no choice but to use me as your quarterback in the second half of today's game. What do you have to lose? Your team lost three quarterbacks today, and you do not have one single person who can play quarterback. If anyone in this room has a different opinion, we would all like to hear it." There was silence. J. C. quipped, "Coach Pitts, listen, please. Be an angel. Let me play, okay?"

Pitts responded, "You're either out of your mind or you truly believe you can do it. Mr. De Lord, you are definitely right about one thing: this organization has absolutely nothing to lose. We do not have a quarterback for the second half. We lost three quarterbacks today. If we play you a couple of downs and it doesn't work out, we'll just yank you right out of the game!"

J. C. offered, "I'm not going to tell you about my past. I suggest that there might be a time in each of our lives when we have to believe that something good will happen despite the fact that all of the odds seem to be stacked against us. You might even say that we must have faith and hope. Occasionally, we have to believe in the possibility of a miracle. Let me tell you what I'm going to do. Let me play quarterback for the first series of downs in the second half. If the Saints don't score, I'll leave the field. For years, it seems like centuries, I've heard people complain that life isn't fair. So, Coach Pitts, what do you want to do? Do you want to lead your team back onto the field with no quarterback, or do you want to take the team back out there with lucky number seven?"

Coach Pitts fumbled with his response, "I've never had a day like this before. Thirty minutes ago, I was convinced that things just couldn't get any worse, and then they did. I am beginning to think that things can only get better. I've already lost three quarterbacks today, and it also looks very obvious to all of us that we are on our way to losing this game. This is the first time in thirty years of coaching football that I have ever made it to the Super Bowl. I'm not going to just give up without a fight. Men—and that includes you, Mr. De Lord—I want to win this game more than I can even say. I don't know if I will ever get another chance to participate in a Super Bowl game. We all know how difficult it is to get this far. I have to acknowledge that, in order for a coach to be successful, he may occasionally have to take a chance. On occasion, a coach might have to try something that appears unorthodox, or he might even have to try something that seems just a little bit crazy. Gentlemen, Mr. De Lord is absolutely correct, beyond a shadow of a doubt. Without him, we don't stand a snowball's chance in hell!"

J. C. really didn't like Coach Pitts's reference to hell, and he glared at Pitts in a cold, disapproving manner.

Pitts continued, "With Mr. De Lord, who knows what will happen? May God help us! Gentlemen, let's go out there and play some football like we never played before. If nothing else, we'll probably catch the Villains off guard. I'm sure they are convinced that we won't even return to the field to play the rest of the game. We're not going to give up yet!"

J. C. smiled, "Amen! Hallelujah! We will play some football like no one has ever seen before!"

There were dozens of players and several coaches in the locker room, each with a different expression on his face. None of them knew what to think. Most of them realized that men in desperate situations often have to resort to desperate measures. The security guard standing just outside the door opened it and blew his whistle to indicate that it was time for the team to go back out onto the field.

Thomas moved a couple of steps closer to Coach Pitts and pleaded, "I seriously doubt he can help us in any way. I think it will be a major mistake if we let him play!"

Andrews walked toward J. C. and looked him directly in the eyes and said, "J. C., you're the man. I believe what you are telling us. We have no other alternative. If you can't do it, then nobody can. Coach Pitts, he's the QB. He's our main man. Give him the ball!"

The two offensive guards, James and John Boom, stood shoulder to shoulder and bellowed in unison with thunderous voices, "Coach, give Mr. De Lord the ball!"

Coach Pitts asked, "Mr. De Lord, what's in it for you? How much money do you want?"

J. C. replied, "I tell you what, I'm just going to do it. I volunteer to do this for nothing. I'm not rich, but I don't need the money. However, I do have a sense of humor. If I fail miserably, just pretend I'm a CEO in the banking industry or an executive on Wall Street and pay me several million dollars. No! I'm just kidding. We don't have time to talk about my motives. I want to be your quarterback for personal reasons. Actually, if we win the game, you can donate one million dollars to a charity organization that the team selects. I don't need to have a profound reason for playing in this game, despite the fact that reporters and scholars might think I should have profound reasons for doing this. Very simply, I have decided it would be appropriate if I helped the Saints win this game."

Pitts picked up a nearby football and handed it to J. C. and yelled to the entire locker room, "Saints! Saints! Let's go, Saints!" Then he implored, "Mary, Mother of God, wherever you are, please help us."

J. C. smiled and raised his eyebrows, "Somehow, I have a feeling that she is not far from here."

The players and coaches merged rapidly in the center of the room and joined hands. Some of the players lowered their heads while others raised their eyes toward the heavens. J. C. volunteered that he would like to lead the team in a short prayer. "Trust in God. Trust also in me. You did not choose me, but I chose you. Together we can be victorious."

One of the Boom brothers interjected, "It is time for all of us to be confident and to stand together as one. This man will lead us to victory!"

J. C. proclaimed it was time for a pep talk, "This is Super Bowl Forty-Four. We are losing this football game by a score of forty-two to three. We have three choices. Our first choice is to just concede and not go back out to play the second half of this game. If so, we lose. Our second choice is to get back on the field and just go through the motions of playing football. If we do this, we will lose." With even more enthusiasm, he continued, "Finally, our third choice is to play the game and reach for the stars! There will only be one Super Bowl Forty-Four, and this will definitely be the only time that some of you will ever have the opportunity to play in a Super Bowl. I stand here in front of you, and I beg you to realize the third choice is really the only choice we have. Let's dig down deep into our hearts and souls. Let's go out there and play some inspired football and kick some butt. Let's go Saints!" J. C. closed with, *"In aeternum te amabo."* Simon asked what he'd said and J. C. explained it meant "I will love you for all eternity."

The players' fists pumped in unison as they chanted "Saints! Saints! Let's go Saints!" As the chanting continued, Coach Pitts asked J. C., Rocky, and Thomas to accompany him to a nearby office. They entered the office and Pitts broke the news. "Hope Evig has been kidnapped, and the kidnappers have demanded that a ransom of one million dollars be paid before the second half begins. It is my understanding that efforts are being made to gather the ransom money, and it will be delivered shortly." Both Rocky and Thomas reacted with cursing, arm-waving, and frenetic gesticulations. J. C. reacted in a more subdued manner. "I know who Hope is," he said. "I think I might have seen a picture of her in the newspaper. I saw her enter a utility room with two men about twenty minutes ago." J. C. provided instructions, "Coach Pitts, please have three of our big guys head over to that utility room and put a stop to this kidnapping nonsense. I'm thinking that Sam Sprigs can lead the way. If I were a kidnapper, I wouldn't want to see Mr. Sprigs coming after me. In fact, even if I wasn't a kidnapper, I wouldn't want to see Mr. Sprigs coming after me. I suggest he take a couple of our other big guys with him, maybe George Giles and Nate Bartholomew. I overheard one of the men named Guido say to Hope that they didn't actually have any weapons. I can explain how to get to the room."

The three men stared at J. C. in a confounded manner, and Pitts whispered, "Mr. De Lord, you are just full of surprises. Let's see if we can rescue Hope and then go back out there and play some serious football."

J. C. said, "I have to say something. With respect to the information I just gave you on the kidnappers, it may seem that I am ubiquitous and omniscient. The fact of the matter is I just happened to be in the right place at the right time. Frequently, the answer to a difficult problem in life is relatively simple."

It didn't take long for J. C. to provide Sprigs with clear directions to the utility room, and Sprigs replied, "We're on our way. Amen!"

Sprigs, Giles, and Bartholomew raced out of the locker room and to the locked door, which they collectively began to batter down. Within seconds the door opened, almost coming off its hinges. Sprigs looked directly at Vince and informed him authoritatively, "This kidnapping attempt is over! Amen!"

Vince and Guido were big "tough guys," but toughness is relative. Vince and Guido realized they had no weapons and that a scuffle with Sprigs, Giles, and Bartholomew would only lead to disastrous results. Vince evaluated the circumstances and provided his immediate concurrence. He said, "Okay. There are occasions where a quick surrender is the better part of valor."

Guido made a quick and intelligent decision and chimed in, "It's okay with me too, boss!"

Sprigs put a muscular arm around Vince, Giles put a beefy arm around Guido, and Hope wrapped both her arms around Bartholomew in a thankful embrace. She shouted, "I never thought I would be so happy to see you big teddy bears." The attempted kidnapping was over. Vince, Guido, and Hope were escorted from the room. The vast majority of the money that had already been stuffed into the duffel bags was sorted and returned to the proper cash registers and safes.

The remaining players, coaches, and trainers exited the locker room and returned to the field. As Coach Pitts walked out with his coaching staff, he displayed a faint smile. It was a smile that lacked conviction and displayed grave concern for the next thirty minutes of football.

J. C. and the fullback, Rocky, walked out of the locker room side by side. Rocky volunteered, "J. C., I obviously don't understand what's happening, but I somehow have an overwhelming amount of confidence in you! I somehow feel like we'll be bonded together for the rest of eternity."

J. C. explained, "I have been sent here by my old coach. He's a good coach. He thought you might respect me. I also understand that you have the reputation of fumbling the ball. Even if you're a bumbler and a fumbler, remember, it's the bounce that counts! You will not fumble the ball today in any way that will hurt our team. I know that you will be there for all of us when we really need you!"

Rocky promised, "I'll definitely be there when you need me." He turned and joined his teammates as they returned to the field of play.

When the players and coaching staff had entered the locker room, none of them had any hope whatsoever. It now appeared as though some of them possessed a glimmer of hope. But then there was Thomas, the end, and to the end, he would be full of doubt. J. C. and Thomas were the last ones to leave the locker room. As they walked down the hallway, Thomas approached J. C. and said, "Hey, Brother! I don't know who you are or what you're up to, but I just want you to know that I don't believe anything you say!"

J. C. suggested, "I guess it's just your nature to be skeptical and doubtful. But you did call me 'Brother.' I recommend that you just wait and see what happens in the next few minutes, and then you too will believe. I have special feelings for those who have not seen yet still believe."

As they walked, Thomas shrugged his shoulders and snarled, "There's no doubt about it. The Saints are going to win this football game today. Is that what you're trying to tell me?"

J. C. responded, "There are many times in life when it is difficult for us to just hang in there and keep working toward what we are trying to accomplish. But my answer is emphatically *yes*. This is exactly what I am trying to tell you."

Thomas acknowledged that he was a natural doubter, and he immediately began to talk about some of the challenges and difficulties in life. "We have world hunger, global warming, overpopulation, and mass pollution of almost everything that was not previously polluted. Average Americans have so much difficulty putting food on the table for their families, paying taxes, buying gas, and not being able to afford health insurance. Why do millions of Americans not have health insurance? Who can possibly cure people with medical problems, you or me?" J. C. raised his eyebrows but said nothing. "It is often quite difficult to believe in the achievement of hopes, dreams and aspirations," Thomas added. He consistently doubted just about everything that could be doubted. If it was sunny for several days in a row, he doubted it would ever rain. If it was rainy for a few consecutive days, he doubted the sun would ever shine again. If fact, he routinely doubted that the sun would ever come up again.

J. C. replied, "My only comment is that I often think that mankind should have become just a little smarter over the years."

Thomas said, "Every once in a while, I guess I need someone to listen to me. Thanks for listening. I am going to pray for you!"

J. C. responded, "Thank you, Thomas. I am also going to pray for you. I want what's best for you and the team. There's no doubt about it!"

Thomas said dejectedly, "I don't think we can win this game." Both men continued to walk out to the field to see where fate would take them.

When the players and coaches reached the field, they were informed of the kidnapping and told that the kidnappers had been apprehended and that Hope was safe and had already been returned to the owner's suite, which was now being guarded by several uniformed security guards.

J. C. knelt down on one knee near the end of the bench, closed his eyes, and appeared to go into a deep and private state of meditation. He understood that it was time to lead his Saints to victory. After about thirty seconds elapsed, he opened his eyes and looked up toward the moon and the stars. His serious demeanor changed immediately.

He grinned and sat on the bench for just a few seconds before the whistles blew signaling the start of the second half. J. C. removed his helmet and pulled gently on his right earlobe with his thumb and index finger.

Sons of Thunder and
a Bolt of Lightning

JAMES AND JOHN BOOM were brothers born and raised in the Bronx. They had fiery tempers and impetuous dispositions. They were born about fourteen months apart to a mother who worked her entire life in the garment district. Their father worked at the docks. Their parents had a wonderful and loving relationship, and both of them retired as soon as the brothers were drafted by the Saints. If any couple ever deserved a good retirement, it was Mr. and Mrs. Boom. Their retirement income was now being supplemented generously by their two loving sons.

The brothers were very similar in size, stature, appearance, and mannerisms. In addition, they also had similar voices. If someone wasn't looking at them, he would have difficulty differentiating between their voices. They both possessed booming and authoritative voices. A young neighbor of the Booms, who was in kindergarten at the time, once said to his mother, "If you look closely at James and John, they're the same guy."

James and John were big, bold, and boisterous. But they never hurt anyone or did any damage to anything. As far as anyone could remember, they were always kind, courteous, and gentle, except when they played competitive sports. They always opened doors and carried groceries for the women in the neighborhood. It seemed like they were always helping their mother or father or someone else. If another kid started to bully someone, James or John or both would immediately intervene and stop it. They both attended Syracuse University on football scholarships. Although John went there a year before James, John ended up changing his major, which gave him an extra year of study and allowed the brothers to graduate at the same time. They both played the position of offensive guard in college, and they were both drafted by the Saints. Now they were both in the Super Bowl. John was the right guard and James was the left guard.

Both brothers always seemed to be screaming about everything that happened on the football field. There was a slight difference in their approach to the game. After a play, James would yell out in his Bronx accent, "Did you see that? He pushed me when I wasn't looking!"

John would yell back at James with the same tone of voice and the same accent, "Wha' d'ya expect? It's a football game. He's just trying to do his job, and you're just trying to do yours. Get over it! Just play the game. All you have to do is respect your opponent and always love one another. That's enough. It's that simple."

James responded in his own booming voice, "Okay, I agree with you!" Even when they agreed, it sounded like they didn't. It was always a treat for the other players to hear James and John talking to one another or to anyone else who was listening. But with their voices, it was pretty much impossible to not hear them.

Beatrice Boom was the forever-loving mother of the Boom boys. Beatrice was always in charge and whenever she talked about her sons, she was always charged up, like a bolt of lightning. Beatrice worshiped and adored her two sons, who were her only children. From the moments they were born, she pampered them, bragged about them, and doted on them incessantly like a good Jewish mother should. She was convinced that they always deserved special treatment, and she did her best to make sure her boys always received preferential consideration. She firmly believed that the only reason the sun rose and sank in the sky every day was because of her boys. She took more pictures and videos of her kids than any mother had ever done since electronic and battery-operated recording devices were invented.

Beatrice once calculated that she took 2,412 pictures of the boys during their bar mitzvahs. Beatrice was a large woman, and she went to every single Saints game, wherever it was played. Every single day of the year Beatrice suited up from head to toe with New Orleans Saints' jerseys, hats, pants, jackets, sweaters, headbands, and socks. Although she never wore a helmet, she occasionally wore shoulder pads. On game days, she added smears of black mascara beneath her eyes to make her look menacing, but her look was toned down just a smidgen by large, dangling New Orleans Saints' earrings. Just as she believed her boys deserved special treatment in life, Beatrice was convinced deep down in her soul that her boys would ultimately receive special treatment in the hereafter. Like her sons, Beatrice also had a loud voice, and during every single game, people around her could hear her saying, "Look, those are my boys. They're my boys! God bless them!"

The Second Half

THE SECOND HALF KICKOFF was uneventful. The Villains kicked off. Simon caught the ball on the twelve-yard line and returned it only nine yards to the twenty-one-yard line. Both the media and the spectators throughout the world were already discussing the possibility that this would be the most lopsided victory in the history of the Super Bowl.

The Saints had returned to the field with only a couple of minutes to spare before the second half began. There was a tremendous amount of concern and confusion among the fans, the media, and the announcers as to who was going to try to play quarterback for the Saints. In all of the hustle and bustle, no one even noticed the new player, J. C. De Lord, until he began to do some jumping jacks. J. C. decided he really should warm up a little before he ventured onto the playing field, and he proceeded to do about fourteen jumping jacks. After the fourteenth one, he ran onto the field for the first play after the kickoff. Coach Pitts clapped his hands with enthusiasm as all the Saints yelled words of encouragement. The spectators and the entire world of football were infused with excitement and anticipation. Everyone began to notice a player with the name "De Lord" on the back of his jersey. Everyone was asking, who was this De Lord? Where did he come from? No one seemed to know. The media initiated a frenzied search to try to find out about him. They quickly discovered his name was in the program. The official program indicated that he apparently had not graduated from any recognized college or university, but he had "life experience." How would that help him play football for the Saints? How in the world had the Saints determined that he would be their quarterback? At least a million questions were asked during the thirty to forty seconds that elapsed before J. C. called the Saints into a huddle.

J. C. addressed his teammates confidently, "Isaiah 40:31 says, 'Hope in the Lord will renew their strength, they will soar as with eagles' wings. They shall run and not be weary.' Although I know your plays, we are going to improvise as we go along. This will be our first play: Rocky and Jude will assume their normal positions in the backfield. I'll fake a handoff to Jude, then he will run to the right side of the field without the ball. Then I'll hand the ball off to Rocky, who will run off the right tackle. Believe me, you will all enjoy this play. We'll call it 'one potato, two potato, three potato, four.' Hike the ball on four."

The players stared at J. C. as if he were insane. Several of the players began to question his call. Thomas said the play wouldn't work, Simon said he wanted the ball, and Rocky muttered, "What's going on here?" J. C. rebuffed their concerns and directed his center, James, to go hike the ball. As James and J. C. left the huddle, the other players only had two choices: stay in the huddle or proceed with the play. They quickly broke from the huddle and went towards the line of scrimmage, looking at each other incredulously.

J. C. stepped up directly behind the center and yelled, "Down. Set. One potato, two potato, three potato, four!" James hiked the football to J. C., who adroitly took about three steps and faked a handoff to Jude after which J. C. neatly tucked the ball into Rocky's large and waiting hands. The handoff was flawless, just as it should have been. Rocky rumbled forward about three yards before several committed Villains concurrently made jarring contact with him. Instantaneously, the ball squirted out of Rocky's hands and flew about fifteen yards toward the right sideline. Everyone on the field raced frantically after the wriggling football, except for J. C. and Rocky. J. C. stood right where he had been when he first handed the football off. Rocky, who was in great distress, was on the ground where he had been tackled, and he attempted to stand up while watching the great commotion. The pigskin looked more like the proverbial greased pig.

During the next half minute, Simon, Andrews, the Boom brothers, and James each had his hands on the ball for the Saints. During this same period of time, Hershee, Hobson, Herod, Johnson, and one of the Farmer boys each had a legitimate chance of recovering the ball for the Villains. The fans were oohing and aahing as the football danced and squirted all over the field. In utter amazement, Rocky got up from the turf slowly and just stood there watching as twenty other players tried their very best to recover the loose football. Never before had so many different players attempted to recover a fumble for such a long period of time without any one of them being successful. The ball was only moving a couple of feet at a time, but it was as elusive as the pot of gold at the end of the rainbow. Several players zeroed in on the ball. They lunged at the ball, and it somehow popped up into the air and, like a guided missile, rocketed its way into the open hands of Rocky, who was standing about ten yards away from the twenty players sprawled out on the ground and tangled together from their futile attempts to gain possession of the football. It looked like those players were playing a giant game of Twister.

J. C. shouted out words of encouragement, "Rocky, I told you that you would be there when we needed you!"

There were eighty thousand people in the stadium, but Rocky realized he was all alone with the football at the twenty-four-yard line. He took off running and never looked back during his seventy-six-yard romp to the end zone. He was about fifteen yards downfield before any of the Villains could even get off the ground. Rocky did not have a lot of foot speed, but he had a heart filled with inspiration and a tremendous head start. Approximately half a dozen Villains untangled themselves from the spiderweb of humanity and initiated frantic attempts to chase Rocky toward the end zone. Several of them began to gain on Rocky as if he was standing still, but Rocky was on his way to the glorious end zone. He continued to huff and puff, like the little engine that could, and he ran as hard as he could. The outcome was inevitable. Rocky crossed the goal line just as a couple of Villains reached the two-yard line. *Touchdown!*

The crowd went wild! The decibel level from all the noise surely exceeded acceptable levels on all Occupational Safety and Health Administration (OSHA) measuring devices. The Saints had scored a touchdown on the first offensive play of the second half. It was one of the weirdest and luckiest plays in the history of the game of football. The extra point attempt was good.

The Saints and all of their fans were jumping up and down with uncontrollable excitement! Coach Pitts shouted, "I can't believe we just scored a touchdown," and he kept repeating the same words about ten times in a row.

Sprigs exclaimed, "There must be a God. Amen!" as he blessed himself methodically. Rocky returned to the Saints' bench and the other Saints players greeted him enthusiastically, by embracing him, patting him on his backside, or by smashing their helmets into his helmet, but in a loving kind of way.

Pitts said to no one in particular, "I think we'll give Mr. De Lord one more chance." During the wild celebration, J. C. jogged over to the bench and sat down silently with a satisfied expression on his face, as if he had just delivered more bread to the table in accordance with the directions from his mother.

Rocky went directly over to J. C. and stopped. He looked J. C. right in the eyes and said, "Thank you. Thank you! I will never forget this moment as long as I live."

J. C. responded, "You're welcome. Now help me. I want you to become one of my followers. We have to score some more points."

The score was now forty-two to ten. This one play had taken almost forty seconds, and there were fourteen minutes and nine seconds left in the third quarter.

Henry Hershee went over to the referee holding the football and snatched it from him. He glared at the ball with disdain and contempt. He focused on the ball as he held it between both hands. He squeezed the ball viciously, and it just popped like a balloon. He threw the remains of the pigskin to the ground and stomped on them with his cleats. He spat at the remains and then turned away and trotted back to his bench with a giant frown on his face. The referee threw a flag for unsportsmanlike conduct and removed the pieces of the destroyed football from the field.

The Crowd Is Buzzing!

DO YOU THINK SHAKESPEARE ever thought to himself, *"To be a bee or not to be a bee?"*

The crowd was animated! The excitement and commotion were contagious. But the game of football, like life itself, waits for no one. The Saints kicked off, and the Villains returned the football to the twenty-eight-yard line. On the next play, the Villains' halfback ran left and gained about a yard. Then there were two incomplete passes. It was fourth down. The Villains punted, and Simon returned it to the thirty-six-yard line. It was first and ten with sixty-four yards to the goal line and there were thirteen minutes and twenty-seven seconds left in the third quarter.

The Saints' offensive team ran back out to the field, and they were greeted with cheering, clapping, and deafening support. The Saints huddled, and J. C. explained that they were going to run the same play several times in a row if it worked the first time. Several of his teammates tried to explain that you never run the same play in succession. J. C. ignored them and said that Thomas was going to line up on the left side and run down the field about five yards, then cut directly across the middle and stop. The ball was snapped, and Thomas ran exactly to where he was told to run and immediately caught a pass that J. C. had thrown right into the midsection of his torso. Thomas was tackled immediately, but it was now second down and five yards to go in order to gain a first down. J. C. waved off the huddle and yelled, "David Andrews!" The play began, and Andrews ran to almost the same area on the field and caught the ball for another five yards and a first down.

J. C. motioned his teammates to get ready for the next play. They huddled, and J. C. said it would be Willie Simon's turn to catch a pass. Of course, Willie pleaded, "Give me the ball. Just give me the ball. I want the ball. Give me the ball, man." Willie always loved to talk and talk and talk some more.

J. C. said, "Okay, man! You want it and you got it." Simon ran the same play and turned around just in the nick of time to catch a pass. It was second down and four yards to go. As Willie kept chattering away about the great catch he had just made, the team huddled and J. C. asked Jude if he would like to make a play. Hay just nodded. Once again, the team went into formation, and the Villains were seething with emotion. J. C. yelled out so everyone on both teams could hear, "Same play!" Each and every player on the Villains' team knew where the ball was going. As soon as the ball was hiked, Thomas and Simon went to the same general location as the last play and then continued to run downfield. Jude delayed about two seconds and then ran out about five yards to that same spot, where he turned and caught the ball for a first down. Jude yelled out, "Man! Oh man! This is fun!" Needless to say, the crowd cheered and chanted, "Hay Jude! Hay Jude!"

The Villains were steaming with anger and frustration. Hershee was so irate and red in the face that he resembled a giant thermometer ready to pop. He vowed to himself that the Saints could never run that play again. Hershee cussed and cursed incomprehensibly as he tried to control his emotions. Every player on the Villains' team verbalized to each of his teammates, "Same play!"

It was first down for the Saints on the Villains' forty-three-yard line. J. C. called a huddle and told his teammates, "Guess what? Thomas, Jude, and Andrews, you all go to the same place!" The Boom boys broke out of the huddle and shouted with glee, "All right!" like little kids with squirt guns on the Fourth of July. Obviously, the players weren't just going through the motions. They were genuinely excited. They were bursting with confidence. Just as the huddle broke, J. C. turned to Rocky and said, "Rocky, after the ball is hiked, delay about a second and then run directly to the left sideline and go long on a fly pattern." The team approached the line of scrimmage. J. C. yelled out boldly, "Down! Set! Same play!" Every Villain on the field knew exactly what to do. The ball was hiked, and Simon, Thomas, Jude, and Andrews all bolted toward the same general area in the middle of the field. There was no pass rush. All of the defensive linemen, linebackers, and secondary players converged in unison toward the same area where four consecutive passes had just been caught. They all turned and looked back at J. C., who was standing all alone about five yards behind the line of scrimmage. The Villains were absolutely convinced they had the Saints exactly where they wanted them. There was no way on God's green Earth or on the field's green turf that this play could be successful.

Hershee was the first of the Villains to bewail, "Oh *noooo!*" The stadium was silent momentarily, and his words echoed as if he were at the bottom of the Grand Canyon. Rocky stood all alone near the left sideline at the thirty-yard line. J. C. threw a soft, somewhat wobbly pass in Rocky's direction. Rocky came to a complete stop and caught the ball after which he took off towards the end zone. Once again, Rocky didn't run fast, and he was having difficulty running in a straight line. He was so excited he could hardly run at all. Several of the Villains raced after him, and they almost caught him. But almost only counts in certain games, like horseshoes and tiddlywinks. Rocky rumbled down the field and scored another touchdown! A couple of F-16 aircraft from the halftime show screeched by above the stadium on their return to a nearby Air Force Base, but it was so noisy inside the stadium that no could hear the flyby. The Saints all ran down the field and mobbed Rocky in the end zone. It was a short-lived celebration. Several players looked around for J. C. and discovered that he had already taken a seat on the bench. The conversion was good, the score was closer, and the Saints, just like the F-16s, were "flying high." The Villains fans continued to jeer, hiss, clap, stomp their feet, whistle, and use every kind of body language they could to encourage their team to get it together so they could still win the game.

Hershee was mean and mad. His rage boiled over, and he tackled a water cooler on the Villains' sideline and destroyed it completely.

The commentators for the television network broadcasting the game chattered incessantly to one another. "Did you see that? I can't believe it! Holy cow! Who is that masked man underneath helmet number seven? What's happening here? Where on earth did this De Lord fellow come from?"

The Villains were reassuring one another that the Saints had just gotten lucky. They were still leading by twenty-five points, and the game still belonged to them. The Villains remained positive that they had the game under control and the victory belonged to them. The Villains' coaching staff had already directed their personnel in the locker room to prepare the champagne for their victory celebration.

At exactly the same time, hundreds of miles away, there was joy on Bourbon Street like never before. The beer and bourbon flowed. The score was forty-two to seventeen with eleven minutes and two seconds remaining in the third quarter.

The Traitor and Speaking in Tongues

THE VILLAINS WERE TOUGH. They were proud. They were determined, and they had the resolve to win this game. There were eleven minutes left in the third quarter, and they had the lead, which they would not relinquish.

The Saints kicked off, and the Villains returned the ball to the thirty-five-yard line. Skippy Milano, the quarterback, handed off to Danny McCardle for an off-tackle run, and McCardle gained eleven yards for a first down. But then two short runs of three yards each and an incomplete pass forced the Villains to punt. It seemed to some that the Villains were playing somewhat conservatively because they still had a big lead and they just wanted the time to come off the clock. The Villains' kicker delivered a booming punt with lots of hang time and great coverage, and Simon called a fair catch at the eight-yard line. As the punt was falling into Simon's hands, he yelled, "I got it. I got it. Just get out of the way and leave me alone. I got it!" The clock was down to nine minutes and twenty-three seconds in the third quarter.

J. C. was the first player off the bench to reach the huddle. Rudy Ruddast, one of the backup offensive tackles, was in the game to take Nate Bartholomew's place. Bartholomew had sprained his ankle and was getting taped up on the sideline. It was not clear whether Bartholomew would return to the game. Ruddast was a loner and did not typically interact or communicate very much with his teammates.

He always seemed to be preoccupied with thoughts of his own, thoughts he never shared. During the most recent off-season, several of the players heard rumors that Ruddast was involved in heavy gambling in Las Vegas, but the rumors were never confirmed. There is always heavy betting affiliated with significant sporting events. If a team wins a game by eight points instead of six points, this could result in some bettors winning or losing large sums of money. As the Saints gathered together, J. C. related they would run a play called "F-2," in which Rocky, the fullback, would run through the number two opening. J. C. added this was a simple play that they could all understand. The Saints broke from their huddle and positioned themselves for F-2. Obviously, they all knew what to do with respect to blocking schemes. There was a handoff and Ruddast, apparently, became confused and blocked his man in the wrong direction. Rocky went into the two hole, where he was hit immediately by the defensive end, a linebacker, and the safety. There was no gain on the play. J. C. was perceptive. He thought it almost seemed like the other team knew in advance where the ball was going.

J. C. called the next play. It was an option play: he could either hand off or keep the ball and run to the left. As they lined up for the play, the Villains moved frantically backward, forward, and sideways before the ball was hiked. J. C. decided to keep the football, and he was tackled immediately by Hershee, who did his best to administer one of his very special Hershee Kiss-type tackles. The fans in the stands heard a thump and a couple of thuds as J. C.'s body was driven into the turf. The players on the field heard Henry say, "You go down!" Hershee hit J. C. in the stomach with his helmet and drove him about eight yards sideways before they both fell to the ground. It was a violent and jarring tackle, and no yardage was gained. Normally, a referee doesn't throw a penalty flag when a player makes a hard but clean tackle on an opposing player. What Hershee did wasn't against the rules; it just seemed like it should have been. The field judge and a referee considered throwing a penalty flag but they concluded that they were just being emotional about the hit because they didn't like the way Hershee had brought J. C. down. The referees consulted with one another briefly to determine if any type of penalty yardage should be assessed. Thousands of people had groaned in unison when J. C.'s body went down to the ground. The other Saints wondered if J. C. would ever get off the ground. For a couple of seconds J. C. lay prone on the ground, moaning, "Now, I remember what pain feels like."

Hershee stood over J. C. and shook his helmet back and forth in his left hand while pointing down to J. C. on the ground with his fingers extended from his right hand. Hershee grunted, "You go down!"

But, J. C. hopped right up, smiled, and confided to Hershee, "Please don't worry, I still love you." Hershee smashed both of his hands into the sides of his helmet and walked away with no comment.

A group of fans in Section 112 began to chant, "De Lord! Save us! De Lord! Save us! Please save us!"

It was third down with ten yards to go, and J. C. called for a huddle, where he smiled as he gave the next play. When the Saints moved to the line, J. C. began to shout out the signals. He saw that the Villains' safety was rapidly approaching the line to blitz, and it appeared as though he might run directly through the two hole, which was where the Saints' halfback was supposed to go. J. C. decided to change the play via an audible. For the next ten seconds or so, J. C. barked out signals that sounded like a dog in distress. At first, the signals sounded like gibberish. The players displayed looks of utter amazement. Thomas then realized that J. C. was speaking to the entire team in Italian. To the Villains' players who were on the field, the calls sounded like, "Exfleip, tunkranope, iskabibble, swertawaf, ish qwawishna kwishna." Concurrently, each of the Saints, except for Ruddast, heard words and signals that seemed to be derived from the languages of their ancestors. The individual players heard words in Italian, German, Polish, French, Spanish, and a variety of African languages. Each player wondered how the other players could understand what J. C. was saying. The strange part about it was that they were all being told to block either left or right in order to open up the middle so the halfback could run through there with the ball. J. C. then reverted back to the old, trusty word that everyone understood: "Hike." He handed off to Jude, and much to the dismay of the Villains, who were in the process of surrounding the two hole, Jude ran directly through a large opening in the middle of the field, gaining about eleven yards before being tackled. First Down!

As always, the stadium exploded with chants of "Hay Jude!" The referee's whistle sounded shrilly.

When the Saints returned to the huddle, J. C. explained, "People often hear only what they want to hear in life. Frequently, people understand things better if someone speaks to them in a way that they can truly comprehend. When people from different backgrounds and diverse cultures interact with one another, it is critical for them to communicate with one another properly. Why are we doing this? First of all, I have to call the next play, and secondly, we might as well have some fun."

J. C. chirped, "Sometimes sports are too serious. A sport is a sport. It should be fun!" The players looked toward him curiously. J. C. simply said, "Okay," and everyone heard him in English this time. *Okay* is one of the most universal words, accepted in essentially every language. J. C. called the play, "Zenome von golder skinnitzel," relating that the center would hike the ball on "two, dos, deux, due, zwei, dois, and twee." Very simply, this meant the ball would be hiked on "two." The players were confused and amazed because each one heard J. C. speaking in his own language. Almost without exception, the players rushed to the line of scrimmage with lively steps and appreciative grins on their faces. Doubtful Thomas was beginning to have positive thoughts, while Ruddast cleverly gave a subtle signal to the linebacker on the other team. There was a gain of only one yard and the referee blew the play dead with his whistle.

The Saints returned to the huddle, and J. C. called a time-out. He looked around at his teammates and said, "I guess I'm not surprised, but it suddenly seems like the other team knows exactly what we want to do." He looked over at Ruddast, the right tackle, and momentarily stared into his eyes. J. C. took a step and gently placed his open hand on the back of Ruddast's leg. J. C. called the next play and noticed that Ruddast smirked as they broke from the huddle. On the way to the line, though, Ruddast grabbed the back of his leg and went down in pain. He seemed to be in excruciating pain. He was screaming that he had a major charley horse in his thigh. The referees stopped play, concluding that it was time for a TV time-out. One of the referees, Yves, helped oversee the medical attendants who were preparing to remove Ruddast from the field. As they carried Ruddast from the field on a stretcher, J. C. told him, "It would have been better if you had never played in this game." Thomas, the thinker, suddenly remembered that he had seen Ruddast the night before with some shady-looking characters in the hotel lobby. After just a few minutes, Ruddast was taken into the locker room for treatment, and the trainers quickly determined that Ruddast would not return to the game. Play resumed on the field, and the Saints huddled. J. C. called for a short pass play. After a quick count, the center hiked the ball to J. C., who threw it to Andrews who caught the ball and ran with it for twelve yards and a first down. The Saints were marching on. They were doing just fine and, at this time, they did not need a marching song.

Hail Mary

THERE WERE SEVERAL MORE plays, which led to a couple more first downs. There were six minutes and four seconds left in the third quarter, and it was third down and nine yards to go at the Villains' forty-two-yard line. They huddled, and J. C. said it was time to score. He concluded it was the perfect situation to call the Hail Mary pass play. J. C. said, "The Hail Mary is normally thrown when a team is in desperate straits. Well, that's us! We're in desperate straits." Thomas said he doubted the play would work. When the center hiked the ball, Simon, Andrews, and Thomas ran long to the left side of the end zone, where they congregated with several defensive players. The ball left J. C.'s hand, and it was swirling and spiraling towards the end zone. At the moment he released the ball, J. C. was tackled by one of the Farmer brothers. Initially, the trajectory of the football was similar to that of a satellite launched from Cape Kennedy. The football went into a comfortable orbit then suddenly decided to comply with the prevailing laws of gravity and began to fall from the sky. As the football was in flight, three Villains came off the bench and ran on to the field to prevent the Saints from scoring. The referees threw three or four penalty flags.

It was unbelievable; it appeared the ball was going directly into Simon's outstretched hands, but he was tackled by Mickey Farmer just a half a second before his hands made contact with the ball. The closest referee immediately threw another penalty flag. It was definitely pass interference. The ball hit Farmer's left shoulder and caromed off Andrew's arm, then it bounced off one of the Villains' helmets and to the side, where it went directly into the hands of doubting Thomas. As the play unfolded, it became obvious to Thomas that he would catch the ball. And catch the ball he did, at the five-yard line, and with three more steps he ran it in for a touchdown. The fans looked back towards the other end of the field because they were positive that J. C. would still be lying on the ground. To their surprise, he wasn't there. He had already returned to the bench and was sipping from a cup of water. The penalties were declined. The extra point attempt was successful.

The television announcer, Howard Bigsell, commented to the entire world, "How about that? How do you like those apples?"

The Saints mobbed J. C. to congratulate him as they all stood near the bench during a television time-out. J. C. motioned for Thomas and Rocky to come talk with him. J. C. proudly related to both men, "I believe that Coach Pitts is being handed a note as we speak. Faith has come out of her coma. She is alert and communicating with the doctors. In fact, her television has been turned on, and she is watching the game. The doctors think it's a miracle." Thomas and Rocky jumped up and down while exchanging unintelligible shouts of joy, and then they raced over to Coach Pitts at the other end of the bench. By the time they had maneuvered through the other players and arrived next to Coach Pitts, he had already read the note and was performing his own jump-up-and-down celebration.

At the hospital in New Orleans, Faith felt surprisingly good. She had already had a telephone conversation with her good friend, Hope. Hope didn't tell her anything about the attempted kidnapping. Faith was sitting up in bed with her head propped up by three or four pillows, and she was sipping apple juice through a straw. She was genuinely excited and had just started to watch the game on TV. She had already been awake for almost two hours, and she felt well-rested. A pair of nurses kept coming into her room every few minutes to check on her. One of the nurses, Betty, had already brightened Faith's day beyond belief by suggesting that Faith might soon be the recipient of a plateful of hospital meatloaf and some mashed potatoes. Could life possibly get any better? She felt that she had complete control of her mind, but she also understood that she should take it easy before she tried to jump out of bed and run down the hall.

Faith initiated the effort of saying thankful prayers for almost anything she could think of. She focused intently on the two most important men in her life: her fiancé, Rocky, and her brother, Tommie. She prayed for their success and invoked special prayers for the success of her team.

Faith yelled "Yat!" directly at the television and implored, "Let's go Saints!"

Nurse Betty helped Faith to adjust her pillows and volunteered cheerily, "Honey, it seems obvious that some of those saints have already performed some miraculous things today!"

Three minutes and forty-eight seconds remained in the third quarter. The score was forty-two to twenty-four, and the Saints still trailed.

Defense and the Great Flood!

THE VILLAINS WERE FORMIDABLE opponents. The Saints kicked off, and the Villains returned the ball to the twenty-eight-yard line. First and ten.

Their first play was a handoff to McCardle, who ran off-tackle for about six yards before being brought down to the turf with a jarring tackle by Rodney Ignatius, one of the Saints' linebackers. Ignatius was a talented athlete who had played several sports in high school and college. But football was his game. He didn't mind the bumps and bruises. When it came down to overall toughness, Ignatius had no equal. He once played the majority of a game with a fractured forearm and never complained or told anyone. After the game, he provided a simple explanation to the trainers and a few media personnel who just happened to be standing nearby. He said, "I was already in the game, so I just thought I would stay in the game. Besides, I make a good salary; I might as well earn it." When his coaches heard these words, they wanted to take a picture of him and frame it.

The next play was an end-around play, and the Villains moved the ball about eight yards for a first down. The ball carrier was brought down by the Saints' defensive tackle, "Big and Tall" George Giles from the University of Montana. George was about six feet eight, 343 pounds, and he hadn't missed many meals in his life. As a teenager, George fell off a tractor and injured his right leg. He always walked around with a slight limp until the ball was hiked. As soon as a play began, all traces of his limp disappeared completely.

The next play was a pass over the middle, which gained about fourteen yards and another first down. The Villains were moving the ball downfield. This time, the receiver was tackled by one of the Saints' defensive ends, Jose Aramatia. His teammates often said that the players on the other teams needed a funeral director standing by after Jose brought them down to the ground. He frequently tackled with such force that the players would say he might as well just finish the job and go ahead and inter the tackled player where he fell.

Eight plays, a couple of penalties, and a time-out later, the ball was on the twenty-three-yard line, and it was fourth down and four yards to go with two seconds remaining in the third quarter. The Villains really wanted to put some more points on the scoreboard. The field goal kicker attempted a forty-yard field goal, and the ball went wide to the left of the goalposts. The third quarter ended. Nonetheless, the Villains still enjoyed what seemed to be an insurmountable lead, and there were only fifteen minutes remaining in the game.

The players from both teams hustled off the field to their respective bench areas. The fourth and final quarter would begin after a commercial break. As a result of the missed field goal, the Saints would take possession of the football at the twenty-three-yard line.

Tears are liquid droplets cascading from the soul.

During the break between the third and fourth quarters, J. C. tilted his head back slightly and intently searched the skies off in the distance. He clasped his hands together, intertwining his knuckles. He felt a lonely tear forming in his right eye. It emerged and rolled down his cheek slowly. It seems that tears fall slowly at first and then suddenly dash off to their final destinations. J. C. took a couple of steps backward and focused his eyes on the ground just in front of his feet. The sky turned ominously dark, and the air became eerily still. Just a couple of minutes before the start of the fourth quarter the Doppler radar screens in the nearby television stations began to burst with activity. Five minutes earlier, the Doppler screens had not identified any storms within a couple of hundred miles of south Florida.

There is a weather phenomenon that occurs in Florida where first there is no rain and then the rain comes quickly. A person can be standing in a parking lot in the bright sunshine and see dark clouds off in the distance. Suddenly, a few hundred feet away, a torrential sheet of rain appears. Within a minute, the sheet of rain is a hundred feet away. Ten seconds later, it is twenty feet away. Then the rain just explodes all over as if a waterfall somehow materialized in the sky.

The heavens opened, and the rain fell. The precipitation began as stinging, missile-like probes. After the initial bombardment of invading water pellets, water began to roar down from above in solid sheets. People who witnessed this explained that two distinct sheets of rain, one from the east and one from the west, approached simultaneously and converged at about the fifty-yard line. There was neither thunder nor lightning. There was just rain and lots of it. Torrents of rain fell from the skies through saturating sheets of water. Water, water, everywhere! It could have been raining cats and dogs, but no one would have seen them because the water was coming so hard and so fast. The monsoon season arrived in full force.

It was a deluge. The great flood was here. The playing conditions were horrendous. The referees were thinking about suspending play, something that almost never happens during a football game. The water permeated the atmosphere. Rain fell upon rain. The water molecules in the air seemed to be attracted to one another like miniature moisturized magnets. The rain was stinging and had a coarse texture to it. People scurried to seek shelter. For some unexplainable reason, the rain felt wetter than normal rain. In total, the downpour lasted about two minutes. The threatening rain clouds danced majestically around the sky and then suddenly raced east, where they disappeared mysteriously as soon as they neared the Atlantic Ocean, just a few blocks away. In another minute, the sky was clear, the air was refreshing, and virtually all the signs of foul weather had disappeared.

The television commercial break ended and millions of viewers were returned to the stadium and the playing field. The professional announcers, who always loved to hear themselves talk and were never at a loss for words, realized they could never even begin to explain the weather phenomenon they had just witnessed.

One announcer, Howard Bigsell, did his best to explain to the television audience that a tremendous rainfall had just occurred during the commercial break and that the storm had vented its wrath and was now completely gone. The cameras focused on wet players, soggy fans, and drenched cheerleaders. The ever-bouncy cheerleaders resembled wet muskrats, and some of them started to cry. The tears weren't needed. There was already enough water to go around. The blonde cheerleaders didn't cry. They just continued to smile and tried their best to look as cute as they could despite their running makeup and dripping hair.

It became obvious to all that the game could continue. The players from both teams returned to the field, and the Saints had the ball with a first down and a long ways to go to reach the treasured end zone. Water permeated the playing surface, and, My God, it was slippery. There were only fifteen more minutes of football to be played.

As the players returned to the field, it was readily apparent to everyone that the ground was very slippery. The field was like a rectangular frosty-green cake with an icy topping. The players' shoes had absolutely no traction. It was very slippery indeed. The players and the officials slipped and slid with every step they took. On the way to the huddle, four of the Saints fell down and just got back up again. During the huddle, J. C. bent down and touched his right knee to the ground and then touched the playing surface with his finger-tips from his right hand. He stood up, looked intently at his scarred hands, and called a play. He called a "keeper," or a quarterback sneak. Thomas blurted out, "That's a stupid call. It's not the right call, and it won't work in this situation!" Thomas knew it was first down with seventy-seven yards to go, and his quarterback had just called for a "sneak," which was normally used to gain a yard or two. Rocky's face beamed, and he exclaimed, "This should be interesting!"

The Saints broke from the huddle and gingerly moved toward the football as if walking on eggshells. Thomas could hear the ground squishing with every step. Simultaneously, the Villains were carefully positioning themselves, and they shook the excessive drops of the slippery mess from their cleats as they cautiously assumed their defensive stances.

James hiked the ball to J. C. on three. With no difficulty whatsoever, J. C. took a quick step to his right as all of the other

Saints made futile attempts to block someone. Without exception, every single one of them fell to the ground without blocking a single Villain. It didn't matter that their attempted blocks were not properly executed. Every single Villain, blocked or unblocked, managed to take only a step or two toward J. C. before they all lost their balance and fell helplessly to the ground. The players from both sides were slipping and sliding and flipping and flopping as if the bottoms of their shoes had been sprayed with WD-40 oil. J. C. was the only exception. He was the only player who seemed to have special shoes. He started moving forward as if he were wearing ice skates, gliding proficiently, and he floated toward the end zone as if he were in a hockey rink. After moving to his right, he changed direction and glided slowly to his left at about three-quarters speed. For J. C., it was like a stroll in the park. He went through the left tackle hole and two Villains closed in on him, but they smashed directly into one another and both went down into the quagmire. J. C. somehow was able to come to a complete stop, as if his body was being controlled by some remote control device. Then he took off again. His feet glided over the slippery surface but, miraculously, his feet remained in constant contact with the ground. His lower body motions resembled those of a speed skater in the Winter Olympics. He churned his legs back and forth, traveling a yard or two with every leg movement. J. C. was the only man standing. Meanwhile, there were twenty-one other players on the field flopping around like fish out of water. As they tried to stand up, they immediately returned to sprawling on the ground.

J. C. passed the line of scrimmage, the twenty-three-yard line, and was at the forty-yard line in just a few seconds. Again, without exception, all of the other players on both teams remained helplessly on the ground. They tried and tried to stand up, but their persistent efforts failed. Several of the Saints continued to try to block someone but couldn't even get out of their own way. Thomas shouted, "This is not working. I can't block anyone." The Villains did everything humanly possible to get up and chase down J. C. As quickly as they stood, they were back on their backsides a second or two later.

J. C. glided to midfield, slowed down, and began to trot toward the end zone at about half speed, not wanting to lose his footing while he was so far ahead of all the Villains. The other Saints just gave up and watched. They lay in their supine positions and just admired J. C. as he pursued his mission to score. For some reason, J. C.'s shoes had their own "souls" with some kind of super-glue mixture on the bottom.

The Villains continued to struggle while trying to help one another stand up, but their individual and collective efforts were to no avail. At the pace J. C. was moving, he was traveling five yards every two seconds. Therefore, even though he was moving forward in a straight line, it took him about thirty seconds to reach the cherished goal line. All of the Saints were still back around the original line of scrimmage, the twenty-three yard line; some of them had actually stood up. They cried out in exaltation and waved their arms jubilantly. Several of the Villains had miraculously traversed the playing field to about midfield, but it didn't matter. Henry Hershee lay prone on the ground at exactly midfield. He was cussing and cursing, and he looked like a giant version of SpongeBob SquarePants. When J. C. reached the ten-yard line, he proceeded on tiptoe like a ballerina *en pointe*, and he reached the end zone unimpeded. He stepped gently over the goal line as if it was a forbidden obstacle and placed the ball on the ground about a yard or two into the end zone. Touchdown!

A few strong gusts of wind blew through, and the emerging sun shone brightly. The frosty turf topping disappeared by the time the Saints made their extra point attempt. It took a while, but both teams had somehow been able to successfully position themselves for the extra point attempt. All signs of wetness and moisture began to evaporate. The players, fans, coaches, hot dog vendors, cheerleaders, and the field itself dried out quickly. Within just a couple of minutes, the players' uniforms went from saturated to damp to almost dry.

Villains, forty-two. Saints, thirty-one.

There was noise! There were deafening cheers of delight, and wails of excitement filled the air. Fumble Pitts went bananas. J. C. sat on the bench, grinned, and shouted, "Save the wails! There will be more opportunities to cheer."

Thomas approached Rocky and summarized, "I knew that quarterback sneak would work. I knew they didn't expect it!"

Rocky just smiled and said, "Right."

A gentle zephyr stirred the air. Fourteen minutes and twenty-seven seconds remained on the game clock.

Another Sneak

NEXPLAINABLY, THE FIELD WAS almost dry. The Saints kicked off, and the Villains had a good return to the thirty-eight-yard line. Then they ran a couple of successful running plays, which resulted in a gain of fourteen yards and a first down. Then they threw a screen pass, which netted six yards, followed by two incomplete passes. The Villains had no alternative but to punt. They punted, and Simon called for a fair catch at the four-yard line. Simon admitted, "I shouldn't have done that. I really should have let the ball bounce into the end zone for a touchback!" Simon never knew what to do when he made a mistake in life. The Saints had almost the whole field to go. They almost needed binoculars to see the other end zone. The Saints had to move the ball ninety-six yards to reach the promised land, the end zone. The game clock was becoming the Villains' best friend. There were eleven minutes and fifty-six seconds left on the clock.

After another television time-out, J. C. called his team to the huddle and gleefully chortled, "It's time to play first and ten." His teammates looked at him as if he were a little bit weird, and several of them thought that maybe he was from a different planet. J. C. related that the Saints needed to move the ball down the field but that they should also take some time off the clock.

Thomas argued, "Why in the world would we want to take a lot of time off the clock? We're still losing this game!"

J. C. replied, "Men shouldn't worry about time. There is an eternity waiting for you. Most men can't even begin to imagine how long an eternity is. Let me just say it's a long time." He called the play, which would be a hand-off to Rocky. They moved to the line of scrimmage. J. C. handed the ball off, and Rocky ran off-tackle for almost exactly ten yards before he was tackled. The referee placed the football on the ground and motioned first down. The chains were moved. The ball was on the fourteen-yard line.

Football players, coaches, and fans truly understand that most plays during a game do not result in moving the ball many yards. In fact, many plays will result in a gain of only a yard or two or maybe no gain at all. Baseball is called a "game of inches." Football is a game where a team strives to achieve the next first down and/or to score points. A first down is accomplished by moving the ball ten yards after a team starts with a first down. Typically, a team will have four "downs" or plays to achieve a first down. Football experts acknowledge it is extremely good for a team to "grind-out the first downs." This means that a team will successfully move down the field in an efficient and methodical manner. It also can have a positive effect because the team retains possession of the football, lots of time comes off the clock, and the other team, in effect, can't score because they don't have the ball. "Grinding-it-out" means that a team will move the ball a few yards at a time, achieve several first downs, and will, hopefully, score some points via a touchdown or a field goal. It was first down with eighty-six yards to go.

J. C. called the next play, a buttonhook pass to Simon on "set." The ball was hiked. J. C. dropped back only a step or two and Simon ran out about ten and a half yards. As soon as he turned around, the ball was already in the air, headed right for Simon's midsection. He caught the perfect pass he couldn't miss and was tackled immediately. The pass was thrown right in the ole' breadbasket. It was a first down, and the ball was just short of the twenty-five-yard line.

Thomas briefly scratched the back of his helmet as if he were actually scratching the back of his head and murmured, "I see. It's time for ten. It's time for ten yards." Rocky and Thomas looked at each other with wide, effusive grins.

The Saints huddled. J. C. handed off to Jude, who picked up a couple of key blocks as he ran to the right sideline and reached the thirty-five-yard line with just a couple of inches to spare. Since the ball had been touching the twenty-five-yard line when the play began and was now just beyond the thirty-five-yard line, there was no need for a measurement. The Saints clearly had a first down. "Hay Jude" reverberated throughout the entire stadium and in sports bars, restaurants, and homes across the country.

The next play was a hand-off, and the ball went forward about eleven yards to the forty-six-yard line. Of course, it was it was a first down. On the next play, the ball was passed to the tight end, and he ran it for another first down at the Villains' forty-two-yard line. The fans were filled with excitement and the players' emotions were sky-high. J. C. handed the ball off to Rocky on the next play, and Rocky rolled up the middle with both hands wrapped around the ball. He was tackled at the thirty-two-yard line. The referees called time-out, brought out the chains for a measurement, and the Saints had another first down by just inches. As one of the referees signaled it was a first down, the crowd went wild. The fans were witnessing what was essentially "the perfect offense." One play after another resulted in ten yards or more and another first down. Coach Pitts was so filled with exuberance that he thought about pouring several gallons of a green energy drink all over himself.

The Saints on the field were "shaking and baking." They were so hyped up and full of energy that several of them almost ran by the huddle. Simon and the Boom brothers were high-fiving, hand-jiving, and shaking their hips from the east to the west; it looked like a hula huddle. J. C. called the play, a hand-off to Jude, who ran to the left and lateraled the ball to Simon on an end-around play. Simon grasped the ball with all his strength and took off down the left side of the field. For a second it looked like he was going all the way. But, suddenly, a would-be tackler appeared, and Simon was knocked out of bounds at the twenty-one-yard line. It was an eleven-yard gain. *First Down*!

The Villains didn't like the situation at all. The Farmer boys were confused and panting. Hershee was fuming and leaping all over as if he had just jumped out of a hornet's nest. Anger bellowed from the bottom of his throat while he made loud, gurgling noises. He shouted, "Get Saints!" The very next play resulted in a hand-off to Jude, who ran about five yards and fumbled. The ball bounced only once, straight up into the air, and Rocky caught it in full stride and ran another five yards. Rocky was tackled and the ball was placed in the middle of the ten- and eleven-yard lines.

The spectators, in unison, yelled "Hay Jude," and then they yelled, "Hey Rocky!" It was, in fact, a first down.

J. C. announced, "It's almost time to score." The players were convinced that a score was imminent. J. C. took the snap. Jude was blocking in the backfield for a play-action pass. Jude moved closer, J. C. handed off, and Jude coasted to the goal line. He was tackled just before the forward progress of the football reached the goal line. Millions of officials all over the world, including the ones on the field, dissected the instant replay analytically. If nothing else, this game would hold the record for how long it took the officials to determine the proper call. After close to ten minutes had elapsed, which included three TV time-outs, it was ruled that the Saints had a first down with about two inches to go to reach the goal line. It seemed that almost everyone could hear a lone and boisterous fan who yelled, "Hay Jude. Way to go!"

This was football at its best. This was what it was all about. This was what die-hard football fans loved. The next play would be the tenth play of the drive. The *big* question on everyone's mind was: had any football team ever previously had ten first downs during a drive down the field? The Saints had just moved the ball ninety-six yards down the field like a well-oiled machine, and the clock had ticked off six minutes and forty-two seconds. But the Saints had not yet scored a point during this drive. The Saints huddled. J. C. proudly announced, "Now it is time to score!" There was no huddle and J. C. signaled for a quarterback sneak. J. C. took the ball from James, the center, and immediately followed him as they both lurched forward into a mass of humanity. The ball went forward about three inches. He had only needed two inches. *Score! Touchdown!*

The crowd was delirious. In her hospital room, Faith choked briefly on some apple juice. Coach Pitts was on the bench and fumbled several notebooks. The Evig family thoroughly enjoyed a group hug. Somehow, during the second half, many of the Villains' fans had converted and were now rooting for the Saints. Most of them didn't know why; maybe it was because the Saints were such phenomenal underdogs. The Villains still had their staunch supporters, and there were still several thousand Villains fans wearing red devil gear who booed and jeered. There was a big, inflated red devil about twelve-feet tall. It was situated just outside the end zone, and smoke emanated from its nostrils and horns. It was hissing, and J. C. looked over at it with disdain. Suddenly, a rogue bolt of lightning appeared out of nowhere and struck the devil right between the eyes. The red devil exploded, but in a wimpy kind of way. It popped, fizzled, and wheezed as it collapsed slowly down to the ground.

There were five minutes and fourteen seconds remaining. The Villains were still positive they would win the game. Simultaneously, the Saints had no doubt that they could actually win this game. J. C. was their savior, and they were positive he would bear the figurative cross and somehow lead them to victory. The score was Villains, forty-two, and Saints. thirty-eight. There was still enough time left for the Saints to score enough points to win the game ... or was there?

The Saints Kick Off Again

THE SAINTS KICKED OFF deep into the end zone, where a Villain caught the ball and put his knee to the ground for a touchback. The Villains had a first down at their own twenty yard line. Essentially, all they needed to do was make a couple of first downs and take precious time off the clock. The victory belonged to them. They ran to the left for five yards and then ran to the right for three more yards. It was third down and two yards to go for a very meaningful first down. The quarterback threw a completed pass to the left sideline for about a nine-yard gain. It looked like a first down, but several penalty flags had been thrown. Holding was called on the Villains' left tackle, and the ball was placed ten yards backward to the eighteen-yard line. Now it was third down with twelve yards to go. Another pass was thrown and caught. But, the receiver was tackled at the twenty-eight-yard line, and it was fourth down. The Villains punted, and the kick traveled high and far. It was a sixty-two-yard punt. Simon signaled for a fair catch at the ten-yard line, and it was miraculous. It was miraculous because he didn't say anything; he just caught the ball. Once again, the Saints' defensive unit prevented the Villains from moving the ball effectively.

The Saints were losing, but they had possession of the football. It was first down and it was only ninety yards to the end zone. During a time-out, J. C. formed a huddle with his teammates and explained they were going to move the ball and have some fun at the same time. He said that football should be a fun game to play. Before the huddle, he had spoken privately to his center, Danny James. He instructed

James to notify the referee that he would be a center eligible for the next play. During the huddle, J. C. told all of his teammates to position themselves at the line of scrimmage in such a way that their stances would be completely opposite to the way they would normally set up for a play. In other words, they would face in the opposite direction, with their faces looking directly at him, J. C., when the ball was hiked, and then they would all go down the field together in the opposite direction from the way they would normally try to move the ball. The players looked at him incredulously and thought how ridiculous it sounded. James said nothing. Only Thomas, with an exaggerated grin on his face, said, "I think this might work."

The huddle broke, and the players positioned themselves in exactly the way J. C. had suggested. As they took their stances, the Saints were facing J. C. in the backfield, and their backsides were facing the Villains. The referees were totally bewildered but could not think of any rule that would not allow this type of formation. J. C. smiled like a grandmother surrounded by her grandchildren. J. C. was the only Saint facing in the right direction. He took the hike and immediately dashed away from the ten-yard line then raced back in the wrong direction into the end zone while all of the other Saints, except for James, raced back with him. James just stood where he was and exclaimed, "Man, this is back-assward football." As a team, the Villains ran forward, backward, and sideways, all going in different directions. They just didn't know what to do with the imposing backsides staring them directly in the face. After just a second or so, the Villains' defense went full speed toward J. C., their faces lit up with the eager anticipation of a sack and a safety. As several of the nasty Villains were beginning to zero in on J. C. near the back of the end zone, the main Villain, Hershee, came charging at J. C. like a man on a mission, but not before J. C. lofted a pass to James at the twenty-yard line. Hershee shouted, "Your butt is mine." J. C. thought he should perhaps call a time-out to debate Hershee's comment since, in reality, it might be the other way around. As J. C. released the ball, he evaded Hershee, who missed J. C. but somehow managed to tackle one of the referees. James was expecting the ball. Although he caught it, he wasn't used to handling the ball, and he hesitated momentarily before he began to run. The result was that James only gained a couple of more yards. In total, it was a gain of twelve yards, and the ball was moved forward to the twenty-two-yard line.

J. C. spoke privately with James again, and he also spoke to Rocky, after which the entire team huddled. J. C. told them, "Same play." Once again, the Saints went to the line of scrimmage and positioned their posteriors directly in the faces of the Villains. The ball was hiked, and the Saints seemed more organized about things this time as they all lined up and faced in the "wrong direction." Once again, J. C. received the football and immediately dropped back about twenty yards near the end zone. All of the Saints were running backward with him, and J. C. stopped suddenly and handed off to the fullback, Rocky. Rocky just stood there while J. C. raced back toward the line of scrimmage, where he turned around and caught a very wobbly end-over-end pass from Rocky. J. C. ran for positive yardage and went out of bounds at the thirty-five-yard line just before several Villains could converge on him to take him down. *First down*! Only sixty-five yards to go.

The Villains were frustrated, and the Farmer brothers complained to the referees that football couldn't be played the way the Saints were playing. They claimed it wasn't fair that the Saints were purposely moving the ball in the wrong direction yet still ended up with positive yardage. The referees just shook their heads and walked away.

During the next huddle, J. C. announced, "Well, that's enough of the back-assward football." He directed his players to position themselves in the normal manner for the remainder of the game.

Thomas chortled, "There's no doubt about it; some of these guys have posteriors that just shouldn't be seen in public."

J. C. handed off to Jude amid resounding chants of "Hay Jude," and Jude ran the ball to the thirty-eight-yard line. The goal line was still sixty-two yards away, but to the avid Saints' fans, it looked like it was about a mile away. Only a few more seconds of precious time had clicked off the game clock, but it was already time for the two-minute warning and a time-out. It was do-or-die time for the Saints.

Since the Saints were losing by four points, a three-point field goal would not do them any good. They had to score a touchdown. The Villains understood all they had to do was prevent a touchdown and they would be victorious. Incidentally, the Villains were just like the Saints—they had never won a Super Bowl and they still had their fair share of red devil fans and supporters. In fact, it was do-or-die time for both teams.

The Two-Minute Warning

THERE WERE EXACTLY TWO minutes, or 120 seconds, remaining in the game, and the Saints only had one more time-out. During the two-minute warning time-out, Coach Pitts and the entire coaching staff gathered around J. C. and provided him with a tremendous amount of suggestions and strategies, which J. C. listened to politely but completely discarded as soon as he ran back onto the playing field. J. C. knew that he would be the only one who could be responsible for the fate of the Saints. The Villains made a lot of noise as the Saints formed a huddle. With a wide and enthusiastic grin, J. C. explained, "My profound advice is: whatever you do in your lives, do the best you can and be as pleasant as you can be. Life is short! Enjoy it!" He continued, "Okay, listen!" He positioned his fists next to each other, extended his arms straight out, and swayed his hips back and forth. He began to sing cheerily with a surprisingly pleasant voice, "We've got to move it! Move it!" He sounded and looked like a leading character from the DreamWorks movie, *Madagascar*.

Rocky said, "Man, I don't know you."

J. C. responded, "Okay, your comment has been noted."

Thomas interjected mechanically, "I just don't like this. This is no way to play football. I doubt that anything we do will work. This huddle is going nowhere." The referee threw a flag for a delay of game penalty. The Saints marched back five yards, and they now had the ball near the thirty-yard line. It was second down and twelve yards to go.

The Saints rehuddled. J. C. quipped, "We've got to move it! Move it! Are you with me?"

As the players broke from the huddle, several of them sang softly yet boldly, "We've got to move it. Move it! We've got to move it. Move it!" With varying degrees of enthusiasm, the Saints positioned themselves for the play. There was a hand-off to Jude, who ran to the right and gained six yards. Of course, there were resounding chants of "Hay Jude" that could be heard throughout the entire stadium and in sports bars and pubs throughout the world. It was third down and six. The clock kept ticking.

Since the play was successful, the Saints seemed to become more alive, including several of the players who hadn't yet been giving one hundred percent. They grouped together for the next play. J. C. half-sang and half-whistled the old tune, "Whistle while you work! Whistle while you work! Da, da, da, da, da, da, da!" It was almost as if J. C. himself didn't know the words. Who does? Since the players were wearing helmets, it was difficult to see their faces, but it was obvious that they were reacting with a variety of mixed emotions. J. C. called a play, and several of the players broke away from the huddle with Tigger-type bounces in their steps.

Rocky moaned to J. C., "I don't know you. I hope this works."

J. C. replied, "That's the second time you said that."

Thomas went directly to his designated position and mumbled to himself, "Who is this guy, one of the seven dwarfs?"

J. C. grinned and said, "I heard that!"

Thomas sang and then whistled so the entire team could hear, "Whistle while you work. Da, da, da, da, da, da, da!" The clock kept ticking.

It was a pass play to Willie Simon, who sang out loudly while the ball was in the air, "Willie! Whistle while you work." Willie caught the ball in the middle of the field, and it resulted in a gain of about ten yards. It was a first down smack-dab on the fifty-yard line. The Saints gathered for the next huddle with less than a minute to go. Several of the Villains could be heard imploring one another to step up their defensive efforts. J. C. sang more enthusiastically than before, "That's the sound of the men working on the chain gang! Oomph! Ah!"

Surprisingly, of all the Saints, Thomas was the one who led

the unified response: "Working on the chain gang! Oomph! Ah!" J. C. called the play, and each and every player bolted to get into position as they collectively sang, "Oomph! Ah!" They sang loudly and proudly. Suddenly, it was like catching a wave. Thousands of fans joined in, as well as the Saints' who were sitting on the bench, the Saints' coaching staff and the cheerleaders. People in homes, restaurants, and sports bars across the nation also sang, "That's the sound of the men working on the chain gang!" When the ball was hiked, there were only eleven seconds left in the game. J. C. threw a buttonhook pass to the tight end, Andrews, for a significant gain of seventeen yards. Andrews did his best to get out of bounds and stop the clock, but he couldn't. J. C. rushed over to the referee and called the Saints' last time-out. It was a first down at the thirty-three-yard line, and there were only three seconds left in the game. There would only be time for one more play.

Rocky approached J. C. and said, "I don't know you, but I'd like to. Also, what are you doing after the game? I'll follow you anywhere."

J. C. responded, "That's the third time you said that you didn't know me, but I truly am quite pleased that you would like to know me better. I truly wish more people would feel that way." He implored his teammates, "Let's go and win this game!"

The Saints formed their last huddle. There was no more singing. It was a very quiet huddle, and only J. C. spoke. It was the first huddle during the entire game that Simon didn't have something to say. The Saints understood that it was really time to get down to business. They formed a large circle, and each player held the hands of the players next to him. Some of them prayed to themselves, and some of them didn't.

The Eagle Soars!

THERE WERE THREE SECONDS left in the game, and the score was Villains, forty-two, and Saints, thirty-eight. J. C. explained to his teammates, "If you never had faith before, you have to have it now. And you should continue to keep the faith forever. We will win this game. Now, very simply, I am going to throw the football down into the end zone." J. C. instructed Rocky and Simon to position themselves on the right side of the center, then he told Thomas to position himself way out near the left sideline. It would be the last play of the game, and the ball was at the thirty-three-yard line.

Thomas and Rocky silently focused on their responsibilities. Simon shouted out to the entire stadium, "Give me the ball. Give me the football, man! Give me the ball." The ball was snapped, and only three of the Villains attempted to rush J. C. The rest of the Villains retreated toward the goal line to make sure that any attempt for a long pass would not be completed. J. C caught the hiked ball in a shotgun formation and moved back a few yards. He stayed in the pocket, and then he rolled left. His offensive linemen did a terrific job of protecting him. None of the defensive players could get anywhere near him.

The Villains only had a three-man rush and the rest of the team was in an exaggerated defense down near the goal line. The only thing the Villains had to do was prevent a touchdown from being scored. J. C. stopped running and just stood there. He held the football in his right hand, near his shoulder. He didn't look right, and he didn't look left. He looked directly up toward the heavens! He proceeded to launch the football about thirty yards down the field and forty yards into the air. Some of the fans noticed that just before the play began to develop, a majestic bald eagle had appeared out of nowhere and landed on the middle of the goal post for a couple of seconds. At the precise moment when the football was snapped to J. C., it was as if the eagle was snapped directly from his lofty perch on the goal post. He soared directly up for about a hundred feet and then immediately swooped down toward the five-yard line like a graceful raptor hunting prey in the wilderness. Mr. Evig knew that his feathery friend had returned. The predatory bird sped toward its prey, the football, and with talons so powerful they could crush a man's arm, he captured the perfect spiral in midair. He secured it for a couple of seconds and then circled over the end zone. Almost all of the players from both teams converged at the middle of the field and stood admiring the majestic eagle with its prey. J. C. remained standing near the thirty-yard line. Rocky, Jude, and Thomas stood spread apart from one another in the end zone. No one else was near them. Everyone inside Sun Life Stadium was standing, and everyone was mesmerized. Not one player on the field was moving. Several fans in wheelchairs bolted to their feet and remained standing to watch the play more intently.

Typically, eagles really don't make much noise, but this eagle shrieked. It swooped away to about the ten-yard line, and then it turned back toward the end zone, all the while retaining possession of its temporary prey. Without warning, the eagle impaled the football with his powerful beak and mighty talons, and his prey literally exploded in mid-air. As the remains of the limp football plummeted from the sky, the sound of silence was heard like it had never been heard before. The explosion of the football sounded like a retort from a powerful rifle, echoing back from every direction. The football exploded into three equal pieces. The eagle shrieked triumphantly and flew out of the stadium. At first, the three pieces flew spastically through the air like confused balloons. One piece of the football went to the left side of the end zone, one went to the middle of the end zone, and one traveled toward the right side of the end zone. One piece went directly to Rocky, one piece went to Jude, and one piece to Thomas.

The first piece of the football fell directly into Rocky's hands. The second piece fell concurrently into Jude's hands. Once again, there were melodious chants of "Hay Jude." For some reason, the third piece stayed in the air a bit longer than the first two. It just hung in the air for a couple more seconds like a miniature celestial body, the full moon in the background behind it. Then it began to move like a falling feather. It danced and wafted through the air for what seemed like an eternity. In reality, only a few more seconds had elapsed.

Everything and everyone was frozen momentarily in time. No one moved on the field. There were three referees in the end zone. They clearly saw the play unfold before them. Finally, the last piece of the pigskin puzzle fell from the sky and landed like a lifeless rag on Thomas's outstretched index finger. Instinctively, each of the three referees' arms extended up toward the sky to indicate that one or more touchdowns had just been scored.

There was bedlam and pandemonium. Confusion and excitement reigned like never before at any athletic event in the history of the world. Obviously, there could not have been three separate touchdowns. The question for the next several minutes, hours, days, weeks, months, and years was whether what had happened actually counted as one touchdown. The officials consulted with one another and engaged in serious conversations and debates. They all had a fantastic time watching the instant replay from several different camera angles. The replay was shown over and over again at the stadium and on television sets everywhere. Then the officials made the final decision. They concluded that there was nothing in the rule book to disallow a touchdown that occurred via an intervention from Mother Nature or possibly an act of God.

Both head coaches and all of the assistant coaches, captains, co-captains, players, policemen, hot dog vendors, cheerleaders, and fans joined in on voicing their opinions while the referees were in the process of making a final decision. There appeared to be more people on the field than in the stands.

About three minutes ticked away before the head official stepped away from the pack of people and signaled a touchdown! The official scorers later determined that Rocky, Jude, and Thomas would each be credited with one-third of a touchdown or two points each. Time had expired on the game clock. The head official blew his whistle to indicate the game was over. People and players inundated the field. The referees concluded there was no need to attempt an extra point conversion. It didn't matter. The game was over! The final score: Saints, forty-four, and Villains, forty-two.

The Stadium's sound system was on full blast!
There were fireworks, laser lights, and streamers falling from above.
There was loud and resounding music:

When the Saints Go Marching In!
We are trav'ling in the footsteps
Of those who've gone before,
And we'll all be reunited,
On a new and sunlit shore,

Oh, when the saints go marching in,
Oh, when the saints go marching in,
Lord, how I want to be in that number,
When the saints go marching in

Lord, and when the sun refuse to shine
Lord, and when the sun refuse to shine
Lord, how I want to be in that number
When the sun refuse to shine

And when the moon turns red with blood
And when the moon turns red with blood
Lord, how I want to be in that number
When the moon turns red with blood

Oh, when the trumpet sounds its call
Oh, when the trumpet sounds its call
Lord, how I want to be in that number
When the trumpet sounds its call

Some say this world of trouble,
Is the only one we need,
But I'm waiting for that morning,
When the new world is revealed.

Whenever there is great joy or sadness, people react in different ways. Coach Pitts screamed, "Hallelujah! Hallelujah!" He laughed and cried at the same time. He didn't know what to do.

Thomas promised himself that he would never again doubt that something good could happen.

Simon collected the three distinct pieces of the football. He raced over and stood in front of a television camera and proudly announced three times, "I got the ball! I got the ball! I got the ball! I'm keeping this ball forever."

Sprigs blessed himself several times in a row and kept repeating, "Amen!" He just couldn't think of anything else to say.

Beatrice Boom looked out over the field and around the stadium and announced proudly to the people standing near her, "James Boom and John Boom, they're my boys! They are my boys!"

Hope and her parents didn't stop hugging and kissing and kissing and hugging.

Henry Hershee melted like a soft chocolate kiss in someone's pocket. He closed his eyes, genuflected, opened his eyes, and walked quietly off the field.

Faith cried tears of joy and turned up the volume on the TV as loud as it would go. She was surrounded by every doctor, nurse, and nurse's aide on the floor, and they all reveled in her joy. Nurse Betty passed out chocolate chip cookies.

Ruddast never played football again. About a week after the game, Ruddast went out to run some errands and was never seen again. A lot of people have looked long and hard to find Hoffa and Bin Laden, but no one really looked very hard to find Ruddast. Later, as the months passed, the rumors were rampant that Ruddast was probably no longer living and his body would never be found.

Rocky was saddened slightly when he recalled that he had moments when he didn't have total confidence in J. C. At the same time, his spirit had been lifted higher than ever by this amazing victory.

Just as the football exploded, J. C. immediately trotted off the field and just kept running toward the players' tunnel, which swallowed him up. Simultaneously, the eagle flew toward the same players' exit but then abruptly turned around and darted back toward the middle of the gridiron. He then split the goalposts like a picture-perfect avian field goal and majestically disappeared over the top of the stadium. First there was a game to be played and then the game was over. When the second half began, J. C. brought a glimmer of hope to the Saints and all of their fans. Now, J. C. had disappeared down the tunnel into the darkness. No reporters or cameras could converge on J. C. for pictures or an interview. He was gone!

J. C. trotted all the way to the entrance of the tunnel that led to the locker room and then slowed to walk. As he strolled down the tunnel to the locker room, he boasted, "Pops, we did it. Amen. Shalom! Shalom to all and to all a good night."

Out of the shadows, a woman stepped forward with a proud look on her face. It was Ronnie, the reporter. She said, "J. C., look at you. You look like a mess. Here, let me wipe your face with my scarf." She proceeded to do so. She wiped his forehead, his chin, his left cheek, and his right cheek. She said, "You did it. I believe that you have given me enough to talk and write about forever. Men and women will never forget you. Thank you."

J. C. replied, "No, I should be thanking you. I have to go. Please tell everyone that I'll see them soon. It's a big universe, and it just seems like there is always something else for me to do." He smiled and winked, and then he turned around and walked away.

J. C. took several steps and then turned his head to his right and said, "Bubba, first of all, my father gave them light. Then he provided water, oxygen, food, and warmth. He also gave them sight, hearing, and the senses of smell, taste, and touch. Then he sent me to help the Saints win a Super Bowl. What more do they want?"

I replied, "God only knows."

Epilogue

VERY EARLY THE NEXT morning, a stadium maintenance worker named Justin noticed something on the fifty-yard line. There was debris everywhere from the victory celebration, which had lasted long into the night, like a Super Bowl New Year's Eve party. The worker was filled with curiosity and discovered what appeared to be J. C.'s football uniform with the number seven on it. It was neatly folded and placed directly in the middle of the field. It was still dirty, and it was partially torn in a few places. There was dried blood on the front of the uniform just below the number seven. The helmet, for some reason, was placed a couple of yards away from the uniform, and it had a large eagle's feather protruding through the facemask. The worker just stood there, shook his head pensively, and smiled. He stared down the field in the direction of the goal post through which the eagle had swooped to help the Saints score their final, game-winning touchdown. To his absolute amazement, an eagle sat there, perched atop the goal post with his mate. Justin looked closer and realized the eagles were in the process of building an aerie on the right side of the goal post. Justin thought the nest really wouldn't bother anyone for the next few months until spring practice began. He picked up the uniform and the helmet with the eagle feather and walked away toward his office.

Two thousand years ago, a son was born in a manger. One of the primary reasons for his existence on Earth was to make God know us better. Another reason was so humankind could know God better. Many people believe this man died so we might live. Then he returned to Earth two thousand years later to help win a Super Bowl.

Several days after the game, J. C. felt like he was in heaven. J. C. thought it had been an incredible experience to play in an amazing football game. He thought he could play in another game sometime. While he had been away from Earth and the years had passed by, he realized he couldn't just sit on the sidelines. He had to get in the game. He had to demonstrate the righteousness of his being. Despite doubtful people like Thomas, he had definitely led his saints to victory. He concluded he truly enjoyed his interactions with Coach Pitts, his teammates, the reporter, and Jimmy, the young boy who had offered him the remnants of a half-eaten hot dog. His camaraderie with all of the people he had encountered reminded him of the fond memories he had of people with whom he had associated with a long time ago. He felt positive that his presence in the game helped God to know us better. Further, his presence in the game also helped the saints and perhaps, all of us, to know God better.

J. C reflected on some of the good times and some of the bad times. He recalled that some men had crossed and double-crossed him. He realized that some people had always supported him. He knew better than anyone that he could forgive those who had crossed him for their transgressions. But it wasn't the time to dwell on the past. It was a fleeting moment in time that called for a celebration. He had played football, and he had made a difference. More than anything else, he wanted to show the world that he cared. He had always cared. He still cared. And show them he did. It suddenly occurred to him that maybe he should get some of the Saints together later that afternoon so they could party hardy. He would make sure there was plenty of beer and wine. And if they ran out of wine or beer, perhaps he could somehow make some more appear. Suddenly, the most important thought occurred to him: he had better tell his mother.

J. C. had not yet decided when he might return for another visit. He just knew it would be sooner rather than later.

ROSTER – NEW ORLEANS SAINTS

Uniform Number	Name	Position
3.	Allmen, Thomas	Wide Receiver
7.	De Lord, J.C.	Quarterback
8.	Sparrow, Steve	Quarterback
9.	Yardley, Jerry	Quarterback
11.	Washington, Zoomer	Quarterback
12.	Matthias, Randy	Safety
14.	Saulston, Jason	Cornerback
15.	Simon, Willie	Wide Receiver
16.	Jode, Brian	Place Kicker
18.	Cupertin, Billy	Punter
20.	Jude, Hay	Running Back
21.	Gold, Gary	Cornerback
22.	Frank, F.	Cornerback
23.	Myrr, Michael	Safety
25.	Agabus, A.	Fullback
26.	Carpus, C.	Running Back
28.	Permenas, P.	Wide Receiver
29.	Rockport, Rocky	Fullback
30.	Andrews, David	Tight End
31.	Ignatius, Rodney	Linebacker
34.	Aqila, B.	Tight End
38.	Silvan, S.	Defensive Back
39.	Timon, K.	Defensive Back
41.	Wiseman, William	Linebacker
44.	Boom, James	Guard
46.	Boom, John	Guard
51.	Matthias, Sam	Linebacker
52.	Artemas, C.	Linebacker
53.	Hermas, D.	Linebacker

55.	Levee, Matthew	Linebacker
56.	Laima, Larry	Linebacker
58.	James, Danny Boy	Center
60.	John, Thomas	Guard
61.	Smith, John	Wide Receiver
62.	Joseph, Timothy	Guard
63.	Kasia, Thomas	Guard
64.	Sophia, Charles	Guard
66.	Ruddast, Rudy	Tackle
68.	Bartholomew, Nate	Tackle
72.	Giles, George	Tackle
73.	Avilla, Terry	Tackle
74.	Sprigs, Sam	Tackle
76.	Aramatia, Jose	Defensive End
77.	Sebastian, Brad	Defensive End
80.	Pope, Tony	Wide Receiver
87.	Philips, Leroy	Tackle
88.	Goliath, Go	Tackle

ROSTER – VIRGINIA VILLAINS

Uniform Number	Name	Position
1.	Jones, P.	Quarterback
2.	Brown, J.	Running Back
3.	Smith, A.	Running Back
10.	Chase, Chipper	Punter
11.	Justthere, Jimmy	Place Kicker
14.	Milano, Skippy	Quarterback
15.	Jackson, Walter	Running Back
16.	McCardle, Danny	Fullback
17.	Johansun, Walter	Fullback
18.	Knowgood, Joe	Tight End
21.	Knotnice, Kenny	Wide Receiver
23.	Congunditis, Charlie	Wide Receiver
24.	Reynolds, Frank	Wide Receiver
25.	Jones, Sandy	Cornerback
26.	Hobson, Hoot	Safety
28.	Johnson, Ricky	Safety
30.	Herrod, John	Cornerback
32.	Johnson, Swede	Tight End
33.	Swanson, Jason	Wide Receiver
35.	Slimeburg, Richard	Wide Receiver
38.	Wagner, John	Defensive Back
39.	Fournier, Rich	Defensive Back
40.	Cotton, Fred	Defensive Back
46.	Farmer, Mike	Linebacker
48.	Farmer, Mickey	Linebacker
52.	Pillotti, Jimmy	Linebacker
53.	Green, Reximus	Linebacker
54.	White, Tommy	Linebacker
58.	Jordan, Jerry	Center

60.	Forbes, Forrest	Tackle
61.	Penney, Paul	Tackle
63.	Ralston, Randy	Guard
64.	Hartling, Rosie	Guard
65.	Middle, Mike	Center
66.	Hershee, Henry	Nose tackle
68.	Krudstone, Kraig	Tackle
70.	Bratton, B. J.	Tackle
71.	Sommeone, Sammy	Defensive End
72.	Donner, Brian	Nose Tackle
73.	Acres, Billy	Defensive End
74.	Barbados, John	Tackle
75.	Lane, Larry	Guard
76.	Street, Steve	Guard
77.	Gearstead, Gary	Guard
78.	Jones, Tyrone	Tackle
79.	Seymore, Samuel	Tackle

Time-Outs

THESE TIME-OUTS ARE PROVIDED for brief diversions. They are not affiliated with the game but might appeal to sports enthusiasts or possibly to anyone in general. Originally, the time-outs were interspersed throughout the story, but they have all been moved to "after the game."

Time-Out #1
Sister Marie and Big Bertha

As she sank into the black muck of the mud wrestling pit, her sweaty 300-pound opponent muttered soft curses in Latin while lying on top of her. Sister Marie thought, *There is no doubt about it, the Pope has betrayed me. He told me that I would have some formidable opponents, but Big Bertha is one tough sister.* It should be noted that Sister Marie wasn't exactly a slouch. At six feet six, 262 pounds, and donning her black-and-white habit, she closely resembled Pedro the Panda Bear at the Indianapolis Zoo.

Sister Marie had every right to exclaim "Oh, brother!" when she glanced over at her monstrous opponent. In actuality, Big Bertha possessed an extremely gentle disposition that antithetically contrasted her physical being, which could best be described as a heaving, moaning, tumultuous mass of adipose tissue. Bertha was a Rhodes scholar and a former member of an elite Shakespearean actors' guild. As a young girl, she had been particularly fond of literature and became especially enamored with all of Billy S's works. When she was a preadolescent she had learned that members of the slender gender seldom played the characters in Shakespeare's plays; at least that was the case back in Big Bill's time. She concluded her only reason for being in life was to play the lead role of Othello, the Moor. She also thought she might like to play the very feminine role of either Juliet or Cleopatra, but despite years of study, she abandoned these dreams at the early age of nineteen, when her budding physique blossomed into a taut, muscular 240 pounds and she received full scholarship offers from the head football coaches at Notre Dame and UCLA. She could have single-handedly defeated a wrestling tag team comprised of true-grit characters such as Romeo, Hamlet, Macbeth, and King Henry IV.

Big Bertha was a concert violinist with the New York Philharmonic Monday through Friday. On Saturday nights, however, Bertha visited the mud wrestling pits, which dearly reminded her of being on stage or "in the pits," as they sometimes used to say of the actors and actresses who worked the early days of the Shakespearean theatre. Being on stage was a habit that Big Bertha just couldn't break.

Speaking of habits, let's get back to Sister Marie. She felt strangely obligated to earn some money so the church could buy a new bingo cage. Heaven knew the church could use a new cage. She felt she had no alternative but to give the wrestling fans their money's worth. In jest, she hurled a handful of mud into Big Bertha's face, and she had the gall to laugh out loud as she did so. Bertha replied, "Oh, yeah. Take this!" And she administered a stunning karate chop to the back of the good Sister's neck. Sister Marie countered by grabbing Big Bertha in a full nelson. Of course, Sister Marie was erudite, and was familiar with her fair share of various classical languages, including Greek and Latin. She screamed into Bertha's ear, "Et tu, Berthus!" as she heard her opponent's vertebrae cracking.

Suddenly, Big Bertha bawled, "What is this, a spot of mud on my new Victorian wrestling shorts? Out, damned spot! Out, I say! How willest I ever cleanse my wrestling trunks?"

Sister Marie chortled, "The same way elephants clean their trunks, with about a half ton of water." Marie thought to herself that Big Bertha's shorts must have been made from an old circus tent. At this point, while Sister Marie had Bertha immobilized completely in a headlock, Marie whispered that Bertha should bring her dirty, sweaty clothes to the nunnery tomorrow and they could throw a couple of loads of wash in while they attended Father Frank Flannigan's Fourth of July barbecue. Bertha softly replied that this sounded really wonderful to her and that she was looking forward to the annual barbecue. She reflected inwardly that she hadn't eaten for some time. In fact, about forty-five minutes had already elapsed since Bertha had polished off her dinner, which consisted of a Caesar salad (her favorite, of course), a chateaubriand big enough for two, a baked potato, fourteen homemade rolls, and a half gallon of Pinot Noir. Bertha knew Father Flannigan's charbroiled burgers were just heavenly. She also knew her enormous appetite would be satisfied completely with a fistful of Father Frank's burgers and a six-pack of suds.

Big Bertha and Sister Marie had been good friends for years. They first met each other at an underwater arm wrestling contest in Fort Lauderdale when they were both sophomores in college.

Back to the wrestling match. The two ladies continued to slip, slobber, and slide in the filthy mud. Bertha picked Marie up over her head for a body slam. Not to be outdone, the good Sister yelled out to the referee, "Double, double toil and trouble, fire burn and mud bubble!"

Big Bertha twirled around three times and launched Sister Marie into the yucky cistern of mud. As her face began to resurface out of the mud, the sister bemoaned, "Father Flannigan! Father Flannigan! Wherefore art thou when I needest thou most?"

A reassuring voice hollered, "I'm over here in the corner of yon ring." Father Flannigan yelled out shouts of encouragement and reminded Marie that it was a wonderful and charitable thing she was doing. He explained that, with the new bingo cage, they could be assured of increased revenue from Tuesday-night bingo, which in turn would be used to build a new wing for the orphanage.

Father Flannigan had a fleeting thought that Marie often had a more ravenous appetite that Bertha. It should be noted that Marie had already asked Father Flannigan if she could operate the new bingo cage and call out the numbers to the crowd on Tuesday nights. She knew deep down in her soul that calling out bingo numbers was the vocation she had always dreamed of. She also knew that calling out bingo numbers in the church basement was somehow oddly similar to Juliet standing on the balcony and calling out to her beloved Romeo. Of course, Father Flannigan realized that if Sister Marie called out the numbers, she wouldn't be in the kitchen eating the food, which meant they might still make a few bucks from the bake sale, which they normally held after bingo play was concluded for the evening.

Once again, let's return to the wrestling match. Marie accidentally kicked Bertha in the shins as Bertha's mind wandered and she dreamt about the ultimate serenity she achieved when she listened quietly to Beethoven's Fifth Symphony. She fell to the ground, writhing in pain, and she noticed the pack of Lucky Nick cigarettes in the sleeve of her T-shirt had been crushed inadvertently. Sister Marie begged for forgiveness, but she also reminded Bertha that she had been pleading with her for years to stop smoking. Bertha just lost it and became absolutely infuriated. She lunged forward and grabbed Sister Marie by the Adam's apple. As Sister Marie began to feign a very believable choking sound, the bell clanged and the match was over. The referee and the judge immediately concluded the match was a draw. At this juncture, the crowd cheered and jeered. Sister Marie and Big Bertha grasped each other's hands and embraced warmly. It was obvious that each one of them truly admired the other's pure, raw physical strength and deeply entrenched sensitivity. Big Bertha waved to the screaming fans and turned to Marie to ask if she would care to join her in her dressing room to share a pot of tea and crumpets. Marie curtsied and replied graciously, "Of course, I would. In fact, I would be most delighted to do so."

Time-Out #2

Thud, slam, wham! Crash, splat, bang, whap, crunch, and *aggghh!* These are some of the sounds we hear and react to during the course of a typical football game. In baseball, there is the distinctive sound of the crack of the bat when it hits the ball, which should never be confused with the sound of a wooden bat breaking. In basketball, one of the most beautiful sounds we experience is the *swish* as a twenty-foot jump shot falls cleanly through the net.

Titus 1:9-13. Surround sound. We are always surrounded by

sound, and we try to block out what we don't want to hear. Saint Paul suggests that we pay attention to sound faith and sound speech.

Time-Out #3

It was the day after Thanksgiving, and it was time for the annual football game between the Hupperyournoz Hozers (that's us) and our opponents from the neighboring town, the Inneryhear Sleezers. This had been an extremely long-standing tradition and rivalry. It didn't matter that both high school football teams played each other every season. This annual "unofficial" sandlot game somehow meant more to all of us. The official game between the two high school teams wouldn't be played for another three weeks. That was just too far away as far as me, Jason, Bunky, Chubby, Horse, and some of the other guys were concerned. The annual battle had to take place to determine ultimate supremacy for the next calendar year regarding which town was better than the other. Harry "The Horse" Hopkins was the only player we had who also played on our high school football team. Our high school football coach knew about the annual sandlot game with the Sleezers and gave strict orders to the rest of his players to not participate in this game because he didn't want any of them to get hurt. At the same time, the coach asked Horse to play in the game because he knew it was important to the town, but he also made Horse promise not to tell the rest of his teammates. The coach knew the chances of Horse getting hurt were comparable to sinking a battleship by throwing marshmallows at it. Horse was about six feet five and had muscles on top of his muscles. The prevailing rumor was that Horse was a freak of nature, and he had only about 2 percent body fat according to the school nurse, Mrs. McGilicutty, who also admitted she just didn't know where to even begin to look for the 2 percent. Our game plan was always a relatively simple one. Yell "hike," snap the ball, and immediately give it to Horse, who, in turn, does his impression of a runaway bulldozer.

Chubby Bentley was another one of our players worth mentioning. He was so fat that it usually took two pennies for him to weigh himself every time he went to the county fair. In fact, the fat man always stared at Chubby in admiration. Perhaps you're familiar with the old saying "He's so skinny that he has to run around the shower to get wet." Well, Chubby was so fat that it was an accomplishment for him just to wedge himself into a shower. Chubby relished his assignment of standing in the middle of the line on defense. If you have ever heard of a defensive wall in football terminology, Chubby was kind of like a defensive building. He really was not very strong, and he was far from agile. In fact, as far as we could remember he had never actually made a tackle. But as soon as a tackle was made, Chubby would be available to jump on the pile. It was just a sight to see. Chubby didn't discriminate; he just jumped on anybody who happened to be on the ground. All of the players from both teams were always trying to hop up off the ground like they had springs on the bottom of their shoes before Chubby had an opportunity to jump all over them. Whenever Chubby landed on you, you tried to get up, but you felt so squished that you thought you just went on a crash diet. Sometimes the players on our team allowed a player on the other team to make a considerable gain in yardage before they tackled him. This was done intentionally because of a mutual understanding between players on both teams. Everyone wanted to make sure that the place where the ball carrier was tackled was far enough away from Chubby so that everyone would have sufficient time to get up from the ground before Chubby came chub, chub, chubbing along and jumped on the pile. All of the players on both teams strongly believed that everyone had to be given at least half a chance to get off the ground before Chubby had a chance to jump on them. Just like in any town, some of the guys in ours just weren't too bright, like Foghead Kozowski. But even he figured out that he really didn't like to have Chubby jumping on him.

Well, we won the game impressively by a score of 174–26. We could have had one more touchdown when Horse intercepted a pass, but he inadvertently bumped right into Chubby who, for some reason, tried to tackle his own teammate at about the ten-yard line. Horse fumbled the ball. It almost seemed as if Horse just threw the ball to the ground intentionally as soon as he realized that Chubby was in the process of landing on him. The Horse took this in stride and volunteered to everyone that he thought it was a good experience for him, and he concluded that everyone had to fumble the ball at least once in his lifetime. With a funny grin and a wry expression, Chubby concurred with him. I'm quite positive that coming very close to tackling his own teammate was certainly one of the highlights of Chubby's incomparable career as a football player.

Time-Out #4
The Commercials

None of us can experience a Super Bowl without talking about the almighty dollar and the new, innovative commercials that are now approaching sponsor costs of about a hundred thousand dollars a second. We should take just a moment to reflect on some of today's sponsors.

Fizzy-Wizzy Bubbly-Wubbly Cola. It not only tastes okay, but it looks great and sounds great too! It's just full of bubbles. And the bubbles are the key. When you drink this bubbly concoction, you become full of bubbles. The result is that you can't eat. If you try to eat, you will probably become deathly ill. Therefore, Fizzy-Wizzy Bubbly-Wubbly Cola is just what you need. It looks great, and it helps you lose weight.

Then there is Beer Here. It's the new kind of beer for when you want a beer and you want it now. Were you ever in the mood for a beer when you were playing cards with the guys, or when you were watching an important game? You find yourself going to the refrigerator and fumbling through the cans of soda and bottles of milk looking for a beer. For several annoying seconds, all you can find is your wife's diet iced tea, several uncolas, some skim milk and a couple of mango-monkey drinks. Finally, all of your problems have been solved. Only two words appear boldly on the can or bottle: BEER HERE. It helps you get the beer you want expeditiously when you're really in a hurry to get back to the tube to see a commercial or to watch tall people fail miserably with their numerous attempts to shoot free throws.

The name of the next product is Take It Now. It's perfect for diarrhea, hemorrhoids, headaches, ulcers, menstrual cramps, and enlarged prostates. This is probably the most important commercial that is shown during the game. If you're one who can't resist all the "fast food goodies" available to eat and drink during the course of a big game, then this is the pill that you need most. Not only does this pill cure virtually anything known to man, but it's easy to swallow. You can insert this wonder pill into almost any aperture or orifice that you can think of. In fact, you can even insert this pill directly into the aperture where most of the commercials on television should go.

Chippy-Dippy Mix. Don't go out and buy a bag of chips and then try to pick out the most appropriate dip for your Super Bowl party. We've got the dip and we've got the chip. We crush old, stale potato chips and mix them into our homemade dip at our Chippy-Dippy factory. When you open the jar, you don't need napkins or plates. Our product tastes great and saves you time and money. There is absolutely no time needed for preparation. You won't soil your hands or clothes with an oily chip. You just open the jar and then use a big spoon to eat the chip-and-dip mixture, which has already been prepared for you and your spoon. At the Chippy-Dippy Company we have succeeded in making life about as simple as it can be.

In summation it is recommended that you:
1. Turn the TV on.
2. Go get your spoon and a jar of Chippy-Dippy.
3. Go to the refrigerator and quickly grab a bottle of Beer Here (which, of course, is provided by one of our cosponsors). Now you are almost ready to go (figuratively speaking).
4. Have another product immediately nearby if needed, and this, of course, should be Take It Now (provided again by one of our cosponsors).
5. Now enjoy your snack, and soon you will be ready to go (literally speaking).

Time-Out #5

In accordance with Christian tradition, there are three virtues— Faith, Hope, and Charity—and they all work together, hand in hand.